SATYR WARS
A Naiad Hope
Volume IV

♦

A Satirical Fantasy for All Ages

Satyr Wars - A Naiad Hope -
A Satirical Fantasy for All Ages
by Becca Bates
Published by Indie Artist Press
Eagle Mountain, Utah
www.indieartistpress.com
First Edition
ISBN 978-1-62522-080-6
copyright © 2016 Becca Bates
All rights reserved.
April 2016

Free Ebook!

Once upon a time...

Get your free ebook copy of
"Faerie Tail" by signing up
for Becca Bates' newletter.
Start Here:
http://beccabooks.weebly.com

1 - The Vampire

YOU COULD SAY this story began when Enya and Jack were born, or perhaps when the oracle[1] spoke a prophecy that fell into the elves'[2] possession. Or you could say that it began when the satyr[3] moved in down the road from the gnome's[4] farm. But for Enya, this story truly began when the vampire[5] showed up on her doorstep.

The knock came as she ate supper with her brother, Jack, and the gnomes that

---

[1] a spirit being known predominately for having visions of the future, all of which come true, though the clarity of the prophecy itself depends largely on the specific oracle

[2] small magical creatures who live in forests and are friendly with fairies; they are especially proficient at making toys, cookies, and shoes

[3] basically a faun

[4] small beings similar to elves in stature, but of a simpler nature; there are many different types of gnomes, and in this context they are farm gnomes

[5] bat-like, nocturnal creature whose main diet is blood; the type of blood is a matter of personal preference

raised them, Olin and Ona. A storm battered the walls and windows of the quaint farmhouse, and at first no one even realized there had been a knock. One of the cerberus'[6] heads lifted and sniffed toward the front door, bearing its teeth with a low growl. The other two heads soon followed suit and it ran to the door, all three of the heads barking obnoxiously.

"Someone's at the door," Ona commented, and all four of them stared at it for a moment, wondering who could possibly be out in this weather. It was rare for them to get visitors as it was, considering how secluded they were, but at a time like this?

"Enya, go see who it is." Olin gave her a nod.

"Me?" She crossed her arms. "Open a door and let the wind blow all of the rain in? With me standing there?"

"Oh, yes, of course," Olin said with a shake of his head. "Jack, then."

Jack stood and went to the door as Enya grumbled that she didn't know why Olin

---

[6] a three-headed hound, known for its fierce protectiveness over its owners and overabundance of drooling

couldn't just do it himself. When he opened it, he saw the silhouette of a being about the size of the satyr down the road, though he didn't think that was who it was.

"May I come in?" asked a pleasant voice, sweet like nectar. "I don't mean to impose, but the storm has become quite relentless, and I could do with some shelter, just until it calms a bit."

"Oh, yes, come in," Jack said, stepping aside to allow the figure entrance.

As he stepped through the doorway and into the light of the lanterns and fireplace, Jack's eyes went wide and the others stared from their seats. He wore a large black cloak that dripped water onto the floor. It concealed most of his form but didn't hide a bulge on his back that shifted slightly of its own accord. Two sharp fangs hung over his lower lip, and the pale grey of his face stood in sharp contrast to his black, beady eyes. Jack was so mesmerized by the stranger that he forgot to close the door until some rain sprinkled on him.

"Thank you for your hospitality," he said with a smile that emphasized his fangs. His gaze scanned the small house and he noticed the family sitting at the supper table.

"Oh, I do apologize. I did not mean to interrupt your supper."

"W-would you care to join us?" Olin's voice came out with a squeak.

The vampire put his hands up. "No, thank you. I doubt you would have anything to my taste. But I appreciate the offer."

"What were you doing out in a storm like this?" Enya said, rising from her seat and putting her hands on the table.

"Just passing through. I've been looking for shelter for a while now, but there have not been any other houses since the rain began."

"You're soaked," Ona said, getting to her feet as well. "Here, take off your coat and hang it by the fireplace to dry." She shuffled over to him and held out an arm to take the cloak.

The vampire shrugged it off, revealing a red lining. Underneath the cloak he wore a tunic, pants, and boots, all as black as the cloak, though the boots were quite muddy. The bulge turned out to be a pair of folded grey wings. Ona took the cloak and brought it over to the fireplace to hang on a nail, though given that it was twice as long as she was tall, half of it trailed along the floor in front of it.

"What's your name, dear?" she asked the stranger.

"Dear?" Enya scoffed under her breath, but the vampire ignored her.

"Cilo. Cilo Lernor."

"Nice to meet you, Cilo. My name is Ona, and that is my husband, Olin." She indicated the other gnome. "And these are our wards, Enya and Jack."

"Jack?" Cilo said with a surprised laugh. "What a strange name."

Jack hunched his shoulders.

Cilo eyed Enya, who still leaned over the table, watching him with a menacing expression. "If you don't mind my asking, what exactly are you?"

Her eyes narrowed. "I'm a naiad[7]."

One eyebrow raised. "Is that so? I thought

---

[7] a freshwater nymph with two forms, a liquid form when exposed to water and a solid form, which Enya typically maintains; in solid form, they have blue, slightly translucent skin and golden eyes, with hair of a texture similar to seaweed

all nymphs[8] died out years ago."

"Not all of them." Enya never took her glare off him, wondering why Ona was being so considerate to a vampire. Not that she had ever met one before, but she'd heard they were untrustworthy creatures.

Cilo shrugged. "Good for you, then."

"Well, why don't you make yourself comfortable out here," Ona offered, gesturing to the front room. "If you don't mind, our food is getting cold."

"I don't mind at all. Thank you." Cilo chose the rocking chair, which was not surprising considering it was the only chair large enough to fit him. It had been built for Enya. When the gnomes had originally furnished the house, they had not factored in raising a creature of her size.

Ona and Jack returned to the dining room and took up their seats, as did Enya, albeit with much reluctance.

"How could you let him inside?" she

---

[8] elemental creatures of many varieties, all of which are female; they are the counterparts to the all-male species of satyr, and when they mate, all female children are nymphs of their mother's race and all male children are satyrs with features that reflect their mother's race

hissed at Jack.

"He said he needed shelter from the storm," Jack replied.

"He's a *vampire*. You can't trust him. And he wouldn't have even been able to come inside if you hadn't given him permission."

"Well it's too late now," Ona said. "And he seems nice enough. Very polite."

"Of course he's polite. He's trying to gain our trust. He'll probably suck us all dry before morning."

"Actually," Cilo called out, "I have a very particular taste I prefer, which none of you contain, and I've fed recently enough to be content. You have no need to worry. I will leave as soon as the storm lightens."

Ona gave Enya a look that said, *"See? Nothing to worry about."* But Enya didn't buy it for a second. She dug into her meal with vigor.

After supper, they gathered in the front room with Cilo, who offered Enya the seat. She shook her head, leaning against the wall near the fireplace with her arms crossed.

"So where are you headed?" Ona asked, picking up her knitting and working with the deftness of many years of practice.

"Cromsen," Cilo answered.

"And where are you coming from?" Enya asked more pointedly.

"Bolur."

"Quite the trip," she said. "Why?"

"Enya, be polite," Ona said with a shake of her head.

"I don't mind," Cilo said. "It's understandable why you would be wary of a stranger. I heard there were many job openings in Cromsen. Work has gotten hard to come by in Bolur."

"What sort of work do you do?" Enya asked.

Cilo shrugged. "Whatever I can find to make ends meet. Odd jobs, mostly. I'm hoping to find something a bit more permanent when I reach Cromsen."

"Well, good luck with that," Ona said, her fingers flying over her work. "It's never easy struggling to make a living."

Cilo nodded. "Indeed. And what is it you do here?"

"We tend to our crops and raise pegasi[9]," Olin dared to speak for the first time. He'd been as wary of the vampire as Enya,

---

[9] plural of pegasus, a horse with delusions of grandeur and wings on its back

though he was much meeker about it.

"I see." Cilo gave another nod. When silence lapsed over the room for a moment, he ventured to ask, "I know it's none of my business, but may I ask how it is you came to have a naiad in your household?"

"Well, the gnomes were allies to the nymphs toward the end there before the final battle[10]," Ona explained. "The twins were born just before the fight, and when both of their parents were killed, they were given to us to raise."

"Twins?" Cilo looked over Jack with a puzzled expression.

Enya had figured out a long time ago that Jack was not really her brother, though no one ever said so explicitly. He certainly was no satyr, appearing more like a gnome in size and stature. For some reason, the gnomes insisted that they were twins, so she never pushed the matter, assuming they had their own reasons for grouping Jack's backstory with hers and pretending they were twins. Whatever the reason, it didn't really matter to Enya. She had been raised

---

[10] the point at which the nymphs and satyrs turned on each other and fought until most were dead

with Jack, and as far as she was concerned, he was her brother.

She crossed her arms. "Yes, twins." Her eyes dared him to deny it.

Cilo offered an amicable grin. "I've rarely met twins. Must be interesting."

They made small talk for a while longer, with Cilo and Ona doing most of the talking, but as the yawns became contagious throughout the family, the storm still showed no indication of lightening up.

"Well, we really should be getting to bed soon..." Ona said.

Cilo smiled, his fangs glistening. "I think I'll be all right out there now that I've had a bit of reprieve." He rose to his feet. "I am most grateful for you hospitality."

"It was our pleasure," Ona said, ignoring Enya's snort at that.

Gathering his cloak, Cilo fastened it around himself and bowed his head to the gnome. "Have a good evening." He nodded to the others and headed for the door with Ona accompanying him, Enya never taking her glare off of him.

"Good luck in Cromsen," Ona said as she opened the door to let him out.

All three of Spot's heads gave a soft growl

as they watched him go.

"Thank you." And then he was gone.

"Good riddance," Enya muttered.

"Enya, where are your manners?" Ona chided, but she did not harp on the matter and they soon were all tucked into their beds. At least for the moment.

2 - Missing Jack

JACK WAS GONE in the morning. Enya discovered this when he failed to respond after she pounded on his door, so she poked her head inside. His room was a mess. A window was open and, though the rain had tapered off during the night, there was a large puddle underneath it. The sheets were haphazardly thrown half off the bed and the pillow was on the floor. Enya dashed into the kitchen where Ona was cooking breakfast.

"Jack's gone!" she cried. "That blasted vampire must have come back and taken him in the middle of the night!"

"What?" Ona ran to the bedroom and stared in dismay at the sight. Enya followed behind.

"I knew we never should have let him inside."

"W-w-what do we do?" Ona trembled. "What did he do with him?"

Enya figured he had probably drained his blood dry and dumped his body somewhere, but she couldn't bring herself to say so. She did not have to. "Look!" She ran to the note she noticed lying on the bed. Among the water stains she could make out the words: *"If you want him back, bring 50,000 larks[11] to the Eight-Headed Hydra[12] Pub in Cromsen in two days."* Enya blinked at the note, confusion filling her.

"What does it say?" Ona asked from beside her.

Handing her the note, she waited for her to read it.

"But... we could never get that kind of money." Ona's voice was wispy and her eyes filled with tears.

"It doesn't make any sense. He saw where we live. What, does he think we're royalty in disguise? Why would he even bother if he knew we'd never come up with that much money?"

"We could sell the pegasi." Now the tears ran freely.

"It still wouldn't be enough. And we'd be ruined." Enya chewed her lip in thought. "I

---

[11] a type of currency equivalent to 172 peks

[12] it's ironic because hydras only have seven heads

have an idea. I don't know if it will help, but it's worth trying." She bent and hugged the little gnome, a rare moment of affection for her, and took the note. "I'll get him back. I promise."

Before Ona could question her, she was out the door and off down the path. They had only one neighbor, and it was a good half-mile to the base of the mountain and another few minutes to reach the cave he had taken up as his dwelling place when he had settled down a couple weeks before. Enya struggled to catch her breath as she pounded on the door he had fastened to the cave's entrance. She heard hooves clomping along the rock floor from behind it a moment before the door opened a crack.

"Oh, Enya," the satyr said, opening the door wider. His goat legs and tail were dark brown and his hair was green with a texture similar to grass, indicating his mother had likely been a nymph of a wood variety, though his age had caused the colors to fade a bit and the hair had began to wilt. His brow furrowed as he took in her concerned expression. "Is something wrong?"

"I'm sorry to bother you, Rhyn," she said between gasps for breath, "but you were the only one I could think to turn to. It's an emergency."

"What is it? Here, come in, sit down." He gestured her inside and guided her to the simple but comfortable straw couch he had fashioned.

Enya collapsed on it and offered him the note. "A vampire stopped by the farm last night to get out of the rain. Now Jack is gone."

Rhyn took the note and scanned it, his eyes going wide. "That's terrible!" He looked past the note at her. "What can I do to help?"

Enya hesitated. "I'm not totally certain, but I thought, seeing as how we could never pay it, and you used to be a Maven[13], maybe... I mean, a little vampire should be no match for a Maven, right?"

Rhyn gave her a soft smile. "I appreciate your vote of confidence. And yes, I'm sure I could defeat him, assuming he was alone."

"What do you mean?" she asked with a

---

[13] before the satyrs and nymphs went extinct, they trained to become Maven, the greatest fighters in all of Terra and militia for the Union, whether they wanted to or not

frown.

Sighing, he said, "Vampires are often hired as mercenaries. They are good trackers. He very well might have been hired out to do this for someone else."

Enya tilted her head. "That seems a bit strange. I mean, they can't even enter buildings without permission."

"Did you give him permission?"

"Jack did."

"I see."

"But why Jack? If he was hired to kidnap someone for ransom, why pick the obscure farm boy with no money?" She tilted her head. "In fact, it would have made more sense to kidnap me, since I might be the last naiad left."

"How are we to know the minds of mercenaries?" He stood and paced. "Well, I certainly can't just stay back while your brother is in danger. We shall go to Cromsen and scout out the place, and I'll see what I can do."

"Thank you," Enya said, filling with relief. "If we take pegasi, we can reach it tomorrow, so we'll have some time to prepare."

Rhyn nodded. "Yes, that sounds good." He paused and turned to her. "Now Enya... I know we only have a short time, and you are quite older than would be typical but, well, you *are* a naiad. I think it would be beneficial to give you a few pointers along the journey in the ways of the Maven so you can protect yourself if anything were to go wrong."

Enya frowned. "I suppose it would be good to have some way to defend myself, but I'm just a farm girl, not a Maven."

"Maven talent runs through your veins. You would probably pick it up quite fast."

"If you think it's best..."

"I do."

"Just a few pointers, then, in case anything happens, like you said. I don't want to get involved with any fighting beyond that."

"I understand." Rhyn gestured for the door. "It's early yet. We should get started."

Enya agreed and they stopped by the farmhouse for a quick bite to eat, a few supplies and rations, and to retrieve a pair of pegasi. After Enya had wished the gnomes goodbye, promising once again that she would bring Jack back no matter what, she and the old satyr took off, soaring over the mountains toward Cromsen.

The first time they stopped to rest and eat, Rhyn told Enya it was time for her fighting lesson.

"It's not just about fighting, either," he said. "We all have a mild fluency with magic as well. Nothing near wizard or sorceress[14] status, but enough to help us out here and there."

"I thought you were just teaching me some defenses," Enya said, her defenses quite high as it were. She was not fond of magic and the thought of learning to use it herself made her a tad queasy.

"Magic can be used for defense as well. For example, I can put a spell around me that gives me a little extra protection. If I am attacked, it won't do nearly as much damage." He waved his hand over his torso and a gleam rippled over him from head to hoof. "Of course, I can't maintain it for long, so it's best to only use when necessary." He snapped his fingers and there was a flash.

Enya winced and backed away.

---

[14] male or female beings, respectively, trained in the ways of magic, typically creatures prone to large magical connections

"Don't worry, it's all quite safe," he assured her. "At least, this part is."

"If it's all the same, I'd rather stick to the non-magic part of it."

Rhyn studied her for a moment. "Are you sure you won't give it a try? Your father was quite natural at it."

Enya's jaw dropped. "You knew my father?"

"I knew both of your parents."

"Why didn't you say so before? When you met me?" Enya put her hands on her hips.

Scratching his head, he admitted, "I'm not really certain. It just didn't seem appropriate to bring up."

Enya dropped her arms and peered at him. "What were they like?"

A far-off look filled his eyes. "They were the top Maven of their time."

When he did not say more, Enya frowned. "That's it? That's all you have to say about them?"

Rhyn took in a deep breath. "It's hard to put into words."

"I always wished I knew about them, more than just that they were Maven."

He met her eyes with a steady gaze. "As I said, your father was a natural with magic, as well as everything else. Your mother was not. She gave everything she had to make it to the top, and ultimately she succeeded. Between the two of them, you're bound to turn out well if you just put your mind to it."

"'Turn out well'? You mean turn into a Maven."

"If that is what you wish."

"Well it's not," Enya said, her eyes flaring as she crossed her arms again. "I wish I was back at home with Jack safe and sound and I never had to leave again. I like it there. It's simple. I have no interest in becoming a Maven. If I get involved, and people find out, then everyone will make a big deal about how a naiad is trying to start up the order of the Maven again, and everyone will have something to say about it. No thanks. I'm perfectly content with being a farm girl."

Rhyn let out an exasperated sigh. "If your parents could see you now, they would be so disappointed. Your mother especially. She worked so hard, pushing herself beyond what she should have been able to do, and you're content to put in the least amount of effort possible?"

Taken aback, Enya's shoulders drooped. "I don't want to be a disappointment to them. But she *wanted* to be a Maven. She fought for it because it was her dream." She straightened with resolve. "I have a different one, one I'm fighting for, too. Once Jack is back home, things can go back to normal. That's my dream, and that's why I'm here, halfway to a city I've never been to with a satyr I hardly know."

"If it's that important to you, then you'd want to be prepared when we get there. That's all I'm trying to do, help prepare you for whatever we might face."

She gave a begrudging sigh. "I suppose that does make sense."

Rhyn stepped closer, holding out a hand in question. "Will you at least try a little magic? Just to see if you can?"

"You say it's all safe?"

"Perfectly. The dangerous spells take conscious effort and much strength, so there is no worry of you stumbling across one."

She tapped her foot as she debated, then let out a reluctant, "Fine."

"Excellent." Rhyn grinned. "Now, the first thing you need is to understand how magic is accessed. Some beings are born with it inherit inside of them, the amount of which is usually related to which type of creature they are. As I said, we have a mild amount of magic, so we can only do simple spells that will not last long. Mavens typically use them to boost defenses and strength during attacks, though we sometimes use them to ease mediocre tasks, such as drawing an item we are having trouble finding straight to us."

He hesitated, his face falling. "There I go, using 'we' as if there were still others besides me." He shrugged the thought away. "Anyway, the point is that there is a resource of magic inside of you that you probably have never used, at least not intentionally. You first have to recognize it and release it before you can use it."

She did not like the sound of that. "Release it? I'm guessing there's no containing it after that point, is there?"

"There are ways, but they are usually used by those with malicious wills to stop another mage from using magic against them. I don't think I've ever heard of it being done voluntarily."

"But it's possible? If I try it out, and don't like it, I can get it sealed away again?"

Rhyn rubbed his neck. "I suppose, if you wish."

She gave a slow nod. "In that case, I'm more willing to give it a shot."

"Good. Now, sit down cross-legged and fold your hands in your lap." She did so. "Close your eyes."

She peered at him and he sat down as well, though the bend of his knees prevented him from sitting cross-legged. He folded his hands as well and closed his eyes. "At the start, it's all about meditation. Try to clear your mind and look inside yourself for a pulsating energy. It might be very small, so it may take a moment to find it, but do not worry about time. Just relax and focus."

His voice soothed her and she found herself lulled into closing her eyes and letting her thoughts float away, something she had never done before. She did not realize that he was using a little of his own magic to help her along. Within seconds, she noticed the pulse he had mentioned. It seemed to be coming from deep inside her chest, and when she poked at it with her mind, it exploded, sending a wave of energy throughout her entire body. She was vaguely aware of a gasp and opened her eyes to find Rhyn staring at her, his eyes so wide she half expected them to pop out of their sockets.

"How did... What... That was you?"

"I guess so." Enya's brow drew down. She did not like how flabbergasted he was. For someone as experienced as him, that must mean she had more magic than he expected, and that simply did not sit well with her at all.

Clearing his throat, Rhyn regained his composure. "Hm. Yes, well, you certainly take after your father then." He cleared his throat again. "Perhaps we should start with something simple, like levitating a small object." He looked around. "See this rock?" He pointed to a rock about the size of her fist sitting a few feet away. "Now, focusing on the energy inside of you, will the rock to lift a few inches into the air. Use a hand movement to guide it, such as this." Holding his arm out toward the rock with his hand out, he lifted it slightly and the rock rose to match. He held it there a moment before lowering it. "Now you try."

Enya repeated his motion, reaching into her chest with her mind to tug on the energy held within. The rock shot into the sky. It took a moment for Rhyn to find his voice.

"Since you seem to have no issue with

amount of power, maybe instead we should try to focus on restraining your energy." He folded his hands in his lap once more. "Let's try meditating once more. This time, I want you to build a funnel around the pulse. Do you think you can do that?"

"I could try," Enya said with a frown. She did not want this much magic running free from her, so she would explore whatever it took to contain it, though she wasn't totally certain what this process looked like. Closing her eyes, she began to focus once more. The pulse was no longer hidden away, so she did not even have to look for it to know where it was. She furrowed her brow in concentration, trying to form some sort of funnel like he instructed, but she had trouble getting anything to work. It felt as though the magic was a fluid, always changing form whenever she tried to mold it. "I don't think I'm doing much."

"Hm. Let's just avoid the magic for now, then."

Enya's eyes snapped open. "That's what I said in the first place."

He waved a hand. "Never mind that. Come, get up."

Both stood and he instructed her on a

defensive stance. She took to it quickly and was soon learning methods of blocking attacks and parrying.

"This is better than all that magic nonsense," Enya said after a while, panting from the effort.

"It's not nonsense, but I see your point." Rhyn looked to the sky. "We should be getting back on our way now. We've taken up enough time here."

Enya agreed and they soon mounted on their pegasi and took off once more.

♦

Jack shivered, straining against the ropes that bound him. For the thousandth time, he wished he'd never allowed that vampire inside. His stomach growled and he wondered if Cilo would ever return to feed him. The door creaked open, splashing light into the dark room and causing Jack to squint against it. Perhaps his thought had been answered.

A shadow blocked part of the light and a hand grabbed his arm, hauling him up and out of the room. He stumbled, his feet lacking circulation. As he blinked at the bright sunlight, it occurred to him that this could not be Cilo, for vampires could never venture outside during the day. His eyes adjusted and he looked to the figure that had pulled him out. It wore a black rubber suit that covered every inch of it from head to toe, and Jack wondered how it got it on, or even breathed for that matter. It was difficult to tell what type of creature it was, though it was about the same height as Enya and gave off a feminine vibe.

Jack's jaw dropped. Could it be her? He had heard rumors of her whispered now and then, but he thought it was just legend—the Black Matron of Death. No one knew for certain who she was or where she came from, but she had earned her name for a reason.

The Black Matron shut the door on the side of the building, where it blended in perfectly with the wall, then dragged him to the other side of the alley. With a wave of her hand, the window on the building they now faced glowed and the image of a different room than he had seen through it before appeared on the other side. Before he quite knew what was happening, she bent and hoisted him through it.

3 - New Plan

BY THE TIME they reached Cromsen the next afternoon, Rhyn had given Enya a few more lessons and she was becoming quite used to the fighting stances. They did not speak much more of magic, except for once when she accidentally let some slip out when performing a parry and knocked Rhyn off his hooves.

"You have to keep a hold on your magic at all times," he had cautioned.

"I wouldn't if you hadn't made me release it in the first place," she had argued with her arms crossed and her nose up.

They had dropped the subject at that point.

Cromsen was a bustling, dirty city, and Enya kept close to Rhyn as she eyed the sketchy-looking occupants scurrying about the streets. She wondered where they were all in such a hurry to get to, and was grateful they had tied the pegasi up a ways away from the city, for she feared they would have been stolen had they brought them inside. She gained many a stare, and wondered if she should have worn some sort of disguise.

"You said it was a vampire, right?" Rhyn asked.

"Yes."

"We should check out that place, then." He pointed to the seediest pub Enya could have imagined. The sign overhead was too faded to make out, but there was a notice by the door that read, "Vampires welcome to enter."

"Makes sense."

They walked in and Rhyn ushered her to a dark corner where they could observe the room without much notice. The pub was rather empty, and it took until after dusk before it really began to populate. A few vampires showed up, but none were the one who had stopped by the gnome farm.

"What if he does show up?" Enya asked. "Then what?"

"We'll keep our distance and observe him, following him wherever he goes. Maybe he'll lead us to Jack."

They waited a while longer, and just as Enya became too restless to wait any longer, the door to the pub opened and Cilo started to enter, paused, stiffened, and rushed back out.

"That was him!" Enya darted for the door without waiting to see if Rhyn followed. Once outside, she scanned the area and saw his black cloak disappearing around a corner. She charged after it and rounded the corner to see him pulling off his cloak to allow his wings to spread.

"Stop!" she cried, reaching out toward him. A blast of energy shot from her arm and pummeled into the vampire, sending him flying, though not through the method he had intended.

"Oof!" Cilo grunted as she ran to his side.

Enya grabbed his neck and yanked him up, her golden eyes glowing with fire. "What did you do to my brother?"

Cilo did not struggle, and she felt him swallow hard against her hand. His eyes were wide and he held up his hands in a placating manner. "Please, just calm down. He's not hurt."

"He better not be."

"I just said he wasn't."

She tightened her grip and he flinched. "Where is he?"

Cilo hesitated. "Did you send that shockwave?"

Enya narrowed her eyes. "Yes."

"Very well. I will take you to him."

She did not relax her grip. "Just like that? How do I know I can trust you? You went to all the trouble of bringing him here and you give up without a fight?"

"My primary matter of business is self-preservation. As such, I prefer not to bring on the wrath of mages." His eyes darted to Rhyn, who had followed behind. "Particularly those who keep company with Maven."

"One who is much more fluent in magic than her, I might add," Rhyn added.

"I rest my case." Cilo's face had paled at that, though his voice still sounded as smooth as ever.

Enya peered at him a moment longer before cautiously lowering her hand, mentally checking her magic pulse to be ready at a moment's notice if need be.

"This way." Cilo turned and walked at a reasonable pace, checking over his shoulder every few seconds to ensure that they were not planning to shoot him in the back with a magic beam or some such.

"Were you hired?" Enya asked as they made their way around a corner.

"Yes."

"By who?"

"Whom."

"The one who hired you," Enya snapped.

"No, you said, 'by who?' and I was saying it should be 'whom,' not—"

"I don't give a jackalope's[15] ass what it should be, just tell me who hired you!"

"I don't know. They wore a hooded cloak that hid their figure and face, and used some sort of magic to mask their scent."

"How did they know about Jack?"

"I didn't ask."

"Why did they want him?"

"Again, I didn't ask. I just did the job I was hired to do, which was to go to your farm, take the boy, leave the note, and bring him here. That's all I know."

"Well you're not much help, are you?" Enya shook her head. A thought occurred to her. "Is your name even Cilo?"

"Of course not. I would never give out my real name on a job."

---

[15] rabbit with antlers, which the animal spends a lifetime trying remove so he can dig a burrow

"Then what is your real name?"

Cilo—or whatever his name was—eyed her, nearly walking into a rubbish bin as he did so. "Why should I tell you that now?"

"Because I asked. Or have you forgotten I'm a mage?" It took everything within her not to blanch at using that term in reference to herself, but if that was what it took, she would make do.

"Fair point. It's Nole. Nole Only."

Enya crinkled her forehead. "No surname then?"

Nole shook his head. "No, I just told you, it's Nole Only."

"So just Nole."

Nole huffed. "Why does everyone have such a hard time with that?" Before Enya could say any more, he stopped walking. "This is it."

She blinked at the wall and jumped into a defensive stance, convinced this must be a trap after all, but Nole touched a brick and a small door swung open.

"I believe we are *too late*," he said, his voice still calm, which only aggravated Enya even more than she already was. She did not know that behind his calm mask, his heart had nearly jumped from his chest when he realized she would not get what she came for, and this was the only way he could think to keep her from lashing out at him in turn.

"What do you mean too late?" She peeked into the room, fear clutching her throat, as part of her kept an awareness of Nole's position lest he attempt to shove her in the room to be rid of her. Of course, Rhyn was right behind them so there was little chance of that. Still, it was best to be wary in such a situation. "It's empty."

"That's my point. He must have been collected by whoever hired me."

"Don't you mean 'whomever'?" Enya said, just to infuriate him because she was at her wit's end.

Nole sighed. "No, you see, in this case it was—"

"I don't care!" Enya grabbed his throat once more and shoved him up against the wall. "I just want my brother back. And you're going to find him for me."

Nole still did not struggle, though he was stiff as a board. "I know you won't want to hear this, so please do not do anything rash, but... I can't."

"You *can't?*" Enya could feel the magic inside

rippling, screaming to be let out.

"His scent ends here."

This gave her pause. "What do you mean?"

"Just what I said. I can smell that he was here, which naturally he would be because this is where I brought him, but then it doesn't go anywhere. I mean, there is the vaguest residue lingering in the direction from which we came, but it's so old he certainly did not go back that way."

"He can't have just disappeared."

"Actually, he could have," Rhyn said. "There are teleportation spells. It's possible whoever picked him up was powerful enough to use one."

"Can you smell whom it was?" Enya asked.

"Finally, you used it properly." Nole squeaked when her grip tightened. "I mean, I'm not sure," he forced out, his voice constricted. "There are a few scents that passed through here, but they all continued on. Then there is a very strange scent that was only in this area. Mostly rubber. I'm not entirely certain what it is."

"That's no help at all." Enya let him go and turned to Rhyn while Nole rubbed his neck. "What do we do now?"

He contemplated for a moment before addressing Nole. "You may go."

Enya blocked the vampire's path before he could leave. "No, I don't think he should. He's the one who got us into this mess. He owes us. So he's going to help us get Jack back."

"Look, I was just doing my job."

"Then you picked the wrong person to work for."

"Enya, he's only assisting us now because we have magic. I'm not certain he can be trusted beyond this."

"He knows Jack's scent. If we can pick it up again, he can lead us to him." She gave Nole a glare. "And he knows what we can do if he tries to double cross us."

Nole gave a nod, his face paling again— beyond his natural paleness, that is.

"Very well then," Rhyn said. "We still have one more chance. The note said to bring the money to the pub tomorrow. Enya can wait within view for someone to come retrieve it while Nole and I stay back and observe." He gave Enya a pointed look. "And perhaps this time you could actually follow my plan."

Enya shrugged. "This method worked, too."

◆

Nothing happened. Enya waited the entire day with a bag beside her filled with stones to give the impression of money, but no one approached her, nor did anyone appear to be looking for the money. It ended up being the same pub they had gone to the day before, so Nole was able to enter and sat with Rhyn in the corner.

"What does it mean?" she asked Rhyn when they had finally called it quits and she joined them.

"I'm not sure." He gave a sad shake of his head.

"It's almost like they never really expected me to pay the ransom. After all, they made it so ridiculously high, how could I have gotten it in time? But it doesn't make any sense. I just wish I knew what this was all about." She slumped in her seat. "And how are we supposed to find him now? They took him away, and we can't even follow, then they didn't even try to come for the ransom. There's no way we'll find him now."

"Actually, there might still be a way." Ryn's voice was quiet, contemplative. "I've been thinking this over while we waited, and..." He took a deep breath. "Back at the final battle, I saw a djinn[16]. Someone made a wish that caused many of the deaths there. I've always thought about going back and trying to find the lamp that must have been left there, but... I never quite had the courage to return. If we could track it down now, though, you could wish for Jack to be brought to you, and all would be well."

Enya and Nole both gawked at his tale.

"You mean to say there is a real djinn?" Nole said.

"Do you really think it would still even be there, after all this time?" Enya asked.

Rhyn sighed. "There's no way to know for certain unless we go look ourselves. But I think it's worth a look. After all, if someone else had found it by now, it would probably have been used in a way that made a big splash, like in the final battle, and we'd have heard about it."

"Good point." Enya chewed her lip. "How

---

[16] also known as a genie, a spirit being who grants three wishes to those in possession of the lamp within which it resides; they have a tendency to be grumpy and sensitive to inquiries about their age

far away is it?"

"A few days by pegasus."

"A few days?" Enya leaned forward. "Jack could be getting tortured right now for all we know!"

"I'm not sure we have many better options," Rhyn pointed out.

"No, I guess not." Enya slumped back again.

Nole cleared his throat. "So... I wouldn't be much help on this quest..."

Enya glared at him. "I already told you, you owe us. You took Jack, and you're going to help us get him back. End of discussion."

He sighed. "I was afraid you would say that. In that case, might I take this moment to remind you that I cannot venture out in sunlight, so if we were to travel for a few days, it would have to be during nighttime."

"Then we had better get started," Rhyn said.

"Now?" Enya said. "I mean, yes, I want to move as soon as possible, but we've been up all day. We'll tire right out."

"Not necessarily," Rhyn said. "With magic, we can extend our ability to stay awake. Just meditate like I showed you and will your body to be refreshed." He closed his eyes and concentrated.

Enya did the same and before long her body bursted with energy, more than she had ever felt before. She hopped up. "Ready then?"

Rhyn frowned at her as he rose. "You really need to be more careful. If you keep overextending magic on your goal, you might cause some accidental damage sometimes."

"Yes, we certainly would not want that," Nole said. "Particularly if it was directed at me."

"I would be so distraught if it was," Enya sneered at him, but she, too, was worried about this aspect. Not for the first time, she wished they had just left the magic bottled up inside of her.

4 - Along the Way

THANKFULLY, THE PEGASI were still where they'd left them. Nole bundled up his cloak and strapped it to his belt, stretching his wings.

"Where, pray tell, are we going exactly?"

"Northwest, to Lake Lucid," Rhyn replied. "I saw the satyr who used the lamp drop it in the lake after he made his last wish."

"Of course it'd be a lake," Enya grumbled.

"I would expect you to like lakes," Nole said. "Seeing as you're a naiad and all."

"Exactly. If I touch water, I turn into a blob of liquid. I can't hold onto anything and it takes some time to change back. It's a bit annoying, really."

"Magic can be used to pocket away items you wish to keep with you when you turn," Rhyn said. "It's something all naiads used to learn as part of their training, allowing them to keep hold of any weapons they had—and prevent them from getting soaked through."

"A helpful tip, I'm sure, but I'm not messing with magic willy-nilly," Enya said.

After Rhyn and Enya mounted their steeds, they took off into the night with Nole taking the lead, using his sonar to guide them through the darkness without incident. More than once, they heard disturbing noises in the distance. Nothing ever approached them, but it set them all a bit on edge.

"We just had to go at night, didn't we," Enya said after a particularly eerie sound.

"No, we didn't," Nole pointed out. "You could have gone during the day if you had just let me be."

"I'm not getting into this again."

"In any case, if you had gone during the day, you would have been seen by all the things in the area. You should be thanking your lucky stars that wyverns[17] are not nocturnal. As such, I've never had the misfortune to encounter one, but I've heard they can be most gruesome, particularly if you find yourself in the midst of a

---

[17] similar to dragons, but with half the legs and twice the temper

poachment[18]. If you'd heard the tales I have, you would not even be venturing out at all. At least, not by flight."

"I've encountered them once or twice before," Rhyn spoke up. "They're not so bad. Much weaker than dragons[19]."

Nole was again reminded that he was keeping company with a Maven, though this was a fact he rarely forgot as it was, and kept his mouth shut.

They made decent progress, despite stopping to rest every now and then, but as the sky began to show the first signs of dawn, Nole began his descent.

"Well, this is it for me."

Enya peered around as she guided her pegasus toward the ground. They were in a large open field amongst rolling hills. "But we're out in the open here. Won't you still be in direct sunlight if we stop here?"

Nole shook his head. "As long as I'm completely covered by my cloak, I will be in no danger. It was weaved with magic specially designed for vampires. It's really the only way we've lasted so long—it can be

---

[18] collective term for wyverns

[19] four-legged wyverns

difficult to find shelter every single day when you can't even enter a building without permission."

"I can imagine," Enya said.

They landed on the ground and Nole untied his cloak, billowing it out.

"Now, if you need me, I'm afraid I'll be unreachable until sunset." He crouched down on the ground and threw his cloak into the air. It landed fully across him, the ends tucking in to conceal every inch of him.

Enya yawned and was about to settle herself down as well, but Rhyn stopped her.

"I want to work a little more on your magic control while we have some privacy."

Enya put her hands on her hips. "Didn't I tell you we should have just let it be? I knew it would be nothing but trouble."

"It won't be, if you learn to control it properly."

She sighed. "I wish at least one thing was simple. Seems like everything has become so complicated all of a sudden. We can't find Jack, we have to go several days to look for a lamp that might not even be there, and all the while I have an overabundance of one thing I never even wanted to mess with in the first place." Shaking her head she said,

"Maybe if we find the djinn, I can just wish it away."

Rhyn frowned. "You can, if you'd prefer, but I'd advise you not to. While it has the potential to be dangerous now, the amount of power you have can be extremely helpful in the future. Like I said, you just need to learn to control it better."

They worked for a little while on it, first trying again to put a funnel around it and, when that didn't work, trying to practice using it in manageable ways. Instead, everything she tried to do was amplified ten times, from another attempt at levitation to an intentional effort to shoot an energy blast like she had done by accident before. When her third shot left a crater in the side of the hill nearby, Rhyn decided they had done enough for the day.

"I think the hardest part to fathom, though, is how you are still that strong now. You've been up for a day and a night, and should have used up much of your magic just during this training session. Yet you still have enough power to do that." He gestured to the indent amongst the otherwise grassy field. "It's quite astounding."

"That settles it, then," Enya said. "After

I've wished for Jack back, I'll use another wish to get a grasp on my magic."

"Just be careful," Rhyn cautioned. "Make sure you know exactly how you want to word it. Djinns can be a tad unpredictable when it comes to fulfilling wishes."

"Of course they are," Enya muttered. "Gods[20] forbid something could go smoothly for once."

They went to bed for the day, shielding themselves from the sunlight with their own cloaks, though not as thoroughly as Nole had done, and were soon asleep.

Having stayed up as long as she had, Enya expected to sleep the entire day away, and was startled to find herself awake while it was still light out. Something rustled nearby and she sat up, turning to see what it was.

"Rhyn, look out!" she cried, shooting a blast at the creature that loomed over his sleeping form. It was thrown back, but so was Rhyn, for she had misjudged the width of her attack. Luckily, he was only touched

---

[20] legendary celestial beings lording over Terra, whom no one has heard from in 16,742 years after a family squabble broke out amongst them

by the edges of it and was merely winded as he blinked in a daze.

Enya jumped up and surveyed the creature sprawled out a few feet away, who did not appear to be breathing.

"What happened?" Rhyn asked, easing himself onto an elbow.

"That thing was about to bite you!" She pointed at it.

Rhyn turned to look and stiffened.

"What is it?" she asked.

"Chupacabra[21]," he spat, rising to his feet. "And if one found me out here..." He looked around. "Enya, you have plenty of magic left, right?"

Enya followed his gaze and saw several more scaly heads barely emerging over the tall grass, all facing them.

"I assume so," she said, sensing the pulse as strong as ever within.

"I've never had to face an entire clubbing[22] of chupacabra before." Rhyn's voice was low. "They must be thirsty for satyr after going so

---

[21] a reptilian creature with sharp spines along its back; like vampires, it also features a diet of blood, but it is especially partial to the taste of satyrs

[22] collective term for chupacabra

long without."

"Do you think we can handle them ourselves?" Enya said. "Maybe we should just take off and fly in the area for a while until Nole wakes up."

Rhyn shook his head. "Then we'd just have to deal with the wyverns, like Nole said."

"Which is easier to take?" Enya asked, eyeing the sun that still had quite some time left before departing for the day. Several dark spots roamed the sky above them.

"At least down here we won't have to worry about controlling the pegasi at the same time, nor plummeting if they are injured."

As they spoke, a few chupacabra dipped out of sight and darted closer, leaving a trail of rippling grass in their wake. Rhyn pulled a pair of daggers from under his cloak. Enya nodded and took up a defensive stance, preparing herself to release another shockwave when the time came.

"You'll be the last resort," he said, holding up an arm in front of her. "Let me handle this as much as possible first. If I get overwhelmed, then you step in. Got it?"

She frowned. "Why?"

"Because I'm a Maven and you've never been in a real fight before."

"True."

She maintained the stance, but worked at bottling up the magic she had awakened. It took everything she had to hold it back now that it expected release. As she did this, Rhyn jumped into action, expertly springing through the air to land on the nearest chupacabra and slice its throat. He dashed to another and stabbed it through the eye when it lunged at him. He fought off three more before the rest rushed forward to overwhelm him.

Enya felt the energy flood her arms as she raised them toward the battle scene. "Get out of the way," she cried to Rhyn.

He glanced up long enough to see what was happening, crouched, and shot himself through the air over the heads of the swarming creatures. Not a moment too soon, either, for a blast rumbled through the clubbing, sending them every which way and razing the grass in its path. As it faded away, Enya and Rhyn stood silent a moment.

"That should about do it," Rhyn said. He wiped his blades on the grass and sheathed them. "Thank you."

"Don't mention it," Enya said, staring at her hands. For the first time since she had tapped into her magic, its presence was not quite as strong as usual, though it was certainly still there.

"I'd best keep watch until dark," Rhyn said. "We would not want a repeat of that. You should get some more rest."

Enya nodded and lay down once more, though she was unable to go back to sleep. She pretended she was, though, so Rhyn would not speak to her, but her mind was too busy musing over all the things that had changed in the last few days, and where on Terra[23] Jack could possibly be. She wished she knew why anyone would wish to kidnap him, and hoped he was still safe wherever he was.

◆

The Black Matron strode through the hall

---

[23] the planet on which they reside, which lies between Olisa and Prow in the Twix galaxy

of the castle to the throne room.

"Where is the boy?" Thero asked when she arrived. He sat on the throne, a dark cloak surrounding him and spilling over the edge.

"In the dungeon," she communicated to him.

"This had better work."

The Black Matron waited for instruction.

"Do you have everything ready for their arrival?" he asked. She nodded. "Good." Standing, he walked to the window with his hands clasped behind his back. "Soon we will have our redemption."

"Yes, Master."

He peered at her over his shoulder. "Ensure that nothing messes this up." Turning back to the window, he held out a hand and it turned into a portal. He stepped through and was gone.

5 - The Full Moon

AS SOON AS the sun disappeared behind the hills, Nole stirred, pushing the cloak aside and stiffening as he sniffed the air.

"Why is there fairly fresh blood?"

Enya sat up. "Oh, it's nothing, really. We just fought off a clubbing of chupacabra while you were asleep." She nonchalantly gestured toward the flattened grass and scattered bodies.

Nole followed her indication and stiffened even more than before. "I see."

"Ready?" Enya asked, rising and stretching.

"I should probably have a bite first," Nole said. Vampires did not need to feed every day, but it was best to do so about once every other day.

"You can have one of them." Enya nodded toward the chupacabras.

Nole wrinkled his nose. "They've been dead for a while. That's disgusting."

She raised an eyebrow. "And eating live bodies isn't?"

"Freshly dead, usually. And I don't eat them." He got to his feet.

"Right, you just drain all of the blood from their body."

"At least you have nothing to worry about, seeing as you don't run on blood[24]."

"What do you need?" Rhyn asked.

Nole sniffed the air again. "I smell a few kitsunes[25] nearby. It should not take long to hunt one down. One is sufficient."

"I'm going with you," Enya said, hopping up.

Nole rubbed at a kink in his neck. "I'll be moving pretty fast. I doubt you could keep up."

She glowered. "All the more reason for me to come. Wouldn't want you running off."

He paused as understanding hit him. "Oh. I hadn't even thought of that."

"I'm sure," Enya said, rolling her eyes.

"No, really. I swear, the last thing I want

---

[24] a nymph's life source is related to their element; in Enya's case, she runs on a water-like substance

[25] nine-tailed foxes whose actual form of communication remains a mystery

is to anger one of you." His eyes darted back to the carnage. "Now more than ever."

"You're still not going alone."

He sighed. "Very well, I will maintain a slow enough pace for you to keep up."

They set off after the kitsune, Enya following at his heels as he sniffed around. Holding up a hand, he brought her to a stop.

"I'm going to lunge forward now," he said in a low voice. "Please do not attack me."

"Fine."

He paused a moment longer, crouching down, then leapt, his wings giving him an extra boost. "Got it." As he returned she could see in the moonlight that he had several tails of a furry creature dangling from his hand.

"Let's get back," Enya said, frowning at it but not complaining.

He nodded and as they returned to Rhyn and the pegasi, he fed on the kitsune, trying to be as quiet as possible to not gross her out. By the time they reached the satyr, Nole tossed the drained carcass aside and wiped his mouth.

"Ready," he said.

They travelled throughout the night once more and as they neared morning, they landed amongst some dunes. This time they passed the day without incident.

"How much longer did you say it would take?" Nole asked after they rose for the night, eyeing the sky.

"Probably another two nights, including this one," Rhyn said. "Maybe one and a half."

"I see. In that case, there is something you should know."

"Oh, what now?" Enya huffed.

"It's just that... it will be a full moon tomorrow night."

"Let me guess," she said. "There's some obscure vampire rule about full moons, too."

"No, not a vampire rule." Nole shifted his weight, scratching his spiky grey hair. "A werewolf[26] one."

Enya and Rhyn stared.

"Let me get this straight," Rhyn said. "You're a werewolf?"

"Afraid so."

"Well that's fantastic," Enya sneered. "Just when I thought things couldn't get any

---

[26] any creature who is infected by another werewolf and turns into an uncontrollable wolf beast once a month on the full moon

better."

"It's not that big a deal," Nole said, putting as much nectar into his voice as possible despite his lie. "Just please don't kill me. And you should probably stay far away."

"Wait, this had better not be a trick to get away from us," Enya said, stepping closer.

Nole backed away, raising his hands. "How many times do I have to tell you? I don't want to be on your bad side. Hence why I warned you an entire night in advance. Besides, I'll be pretty easy to notice so you have no worry of keeping track of me."

"Yet of course it'll happen just in time to delay us one day."

"I don't exactly have a choice in the matter."

"I've heard rumors of werewolves turning back in certain circumstances," Rhyn spoke up, "though no one has ever figured out what it was that caused it per se. Have you ever been able to?"

"Never."

"Then I suppose we'll just have to wait it out."

Everyone was on edge that night into the

next day. As Nole settled down for the morning, he cleared his throat.

"There is one other small matter."

"What now?" Enya sighed.

"The transformation doesn't take my clothing into account, so... I'm just going to leave them under my cloak lest they are torn when I change. Just thought you should be aware."

"Thanks for the warning."

He hunkered down under the cloak, and this time there was some rustling around before he went still.

That evening, as Enya and Rhyn watched the sun go down, Enya asked, "What exactly are we going to do while he's a rampaging beast?"

"Stay back."

She sighed.

"We could have always left him back in Cromsen, you know," Rhyn said.

"If I had known about this, maybe I would have. I just thought his nose could help us track down Jack."

"I'm sure we could handle it on our own if you did not wish to wait for him to turn back."

Enya considered this. "I would like to get

to the lamp as soon as possible."

"And with the lamp, you would not need his nose. You would just wish Jack there."

"*If* it's even there. If it's not, then we would benefit from having Nole with us still."

"So what do you say? Wait one more day in case the lamp is not there, or move on in hopes that it will be?"

Enya thought it over. After a moment, she gave a long sigh. "I guess I'd rather have all options covered. It's been years since you saw the lamp there. We really can't know that it's still there. And if it's not, we have no other leads. It's still a long shot even with Nole, but at least it's something."

"Very well then."

The sun hid itself from their sight, the full moon all too eager to take its place, and a rumble came from under Nole's cloak.

"Let's take to the air," Rhyn said.

The two of them hopped on their pegasi and circled the ground as the cloak bulged and roiled until it flew off completely, revealing a four-legged shaggy beast with glowing eyes and grey fur. Nole's wings remained on its back.

"Are you sure flying was the best option?" Enya asked.

"I hadn't expected the wings to carry over," Rhyn admitted.

As he spoke, Nole's head snapped up to look at them, drool dripping from his fangs. He vaulted into the air, his wings spreading to push him along, but his larger size weighed him down. His wings flapped rapidly but did little to carry him, and he soon was back on the ground. Howling with frustration, he tromped around the area, keeping under Rhyn and Enya the whole time.

"I have an idea," Enya called to Rhyn.

"What is it?"

"He's tracking us. We can keep going, and he'll follow along. That way we can make progress at the same time."

"So long as he doesn't get distracted," Rhyn said.

"We can deal with that when it comes. At least we can get a head start."

"We had better bring the clothes, then."

Enya led Nole a little ways away while Rhyn rounded and swooped down to snag the cloak, clothing, and boots. Nole turned back and charged at him, but the satyr was safely out of reach before he got close enough to do any damage.

They took off, keeping a slow enough pace for Nole to easily follow, snarling and snapping at them the whole time. They actually made quite a bit of progress before another howl sounded in the distance, catching his attention.

"Is that another one?" Enya asked.

"Sounds like it."

Nole took off toward the sound, howling in return.

"Blast, it's the wrong way." Enya turned her pegasus to follow.

The other werewolf howled again, and Nole seemed to have a new fire speeding him along. They watched as the second werewolf came into view, quite a bit smaller than Nole with no wings but a pair of antlers on its head.

"Is that a jackalope?" Enya asked.

"Probably," Rhyn agreed.

The werewolves reached each other and began to circle, growling in turn before the jackalope one lunged at Nole. He swatted it aside and jumped on top of it, tearing it to pieces.

"Oh. I had thought they would work together," Enya said, turning her face away as a queasiness filled her.

"Werewolves are unpredictable. But they usually fight anything."

Nole lost interest after a few minutes and roamed around for a while before something caught his attention and he took off again, still in the wrong direction.

"Here we go again," Enya sighed. "So much for progress."

Things proceeded much this same way throughout the night, though they saw no other werewolves. Nole preyed on other creatures instead, seeming more interested in ripping them apart than actually eating them.

Eventually the moon left the sky and Nole reared up on his hind legs, arching his back. The fur retreated into his skin, and his fangs, besides his permanent ones, diminished to normal teeth. After a moment, he was back to his typical self, albeit naked. Rhyn landed and held out the clothes.

"Thank you," Nole said as he took them from him. "It's always troublesome to track them down before sunrise. I've gotten burned a few times when I cut it too close."

After he had dressed, he rubbed at his mouth to get the blood off, though some of it had dried. "And thank you for not killing me.

That's always appreciated. I mean that sincerely, though I see where that could have sounded sarcastic." He grimaced and put a hand on his stomach.

"Is something wrong?" Rhyn asked.

"I must have swallowed some meat. Gives me indigestion."

The sun was almost within sight, so he soon cocooned himself within his cloak once more.

"We should still reach it tonight, right?" Enya asked.

"I think so."

"Good. I just wish things would stop getting in the way."

It was false dawn by the time they reached Lake Lucid, without any further issues. The lake was not hard to find, as it shone with the bright glow that gave it its name.

"Where would it be?" Enya asked.

"I think it was on that side of the lake," Rhyn said, pointing. "But it was rather chaotic at the time."

They peered at the lake, but the brightness made it difficult to see anything. As they walked around to the side Rhyn had suggested, a light grew a few feet away from their path.

"Is that it?" Enya asked, approaching it.

"I doubt it," Rhyn said, "but it's worth checking out.

As she reached it, it flew into her hand. "What the—?"

Rhyn's jaw dropped.

"Is that a sword?" Nole asked.

"Looks like it."

Rhyn composed himself. "It's Sauveur." His voice carried a weight to it. "It was your mother's sword, left behind in the battle. Only certain people can use it, so it must be attracted to you."

"But I don't want a sword."

"Too bad. It'll stay with you regardless now that you've found it."

Enya huffed. "Let's just find the lamp."

They walked to the water's edge.

"Couldn't you just get it?" Nole asked Enya. "Do your naiad thing and swim around a while?"

"I told you, I can't hold anything while I'm a liquid. I wouldn't be able to move it."

"Yes, you can," Rhyn said. "You just need to use your magic, the levitation spell I showed you."

"I suppose that could work," Enya said, disgruntled that she could think of no real excuse against it. "But... you two have to go away."

"Why?" Rhyn asked with a frown.

"Because... Remember how Nole's transformation didn't take his clothes into consideration? Well, mine doesn't either."

Nole chortled, which earned him a glare.

"Don't even think about peeking," she said.

"No need to worry," he said. "Trust me, you're not my type."

"What a relief."

"If we had more time, I would teach you to magic them with you," Rhyn said, "but based on how you've been handling magic, I'm not really sure what would happen if it went poorly."

"You said you turn into a liquid when you touch water, right?" Nole said. "If you're so worried about it, just jump in the water and let yourself turn, and the clothes will float, won't they?"

"I suppose. But then they'll be soaked."

"It's your choice."

"Just turn away, all right?" she insisted, then raised an arm as if preparing to strike.

"Or do I have to blast you with magic to convince you?"

Nole twirled around.

"Just focus on that area," Rhyn said, pointing to indicate where she should look before turning away as well.

Enya took in a deep breath and walked to the edge of the lake. Peering at the men to make sure they weren't looking, she turned her back to them and stripped, putting down her cloak on the grass and tossing her pants, tunic, and sword on top of it. The sword jumped back into her hand. Cursing, she put it down again and jumped in the water before it could return.

That familiar but disconcerting feeling washed over her as her skin and hair turned into a fluid, held together in a blobby shape through magic. It occurred to her that she must have always used some magic when transforming, but it must be unrelated to the magic inside of her. After all, Nole had magic that turned him into a werewolf, but he had no energy magic to use with his own will.

She guided herself around the lake, observing the floor and sides for any sign of the lamp. It was not so bright now that she was inside of it. Perhaps she grew accustomed to it when she became part of the lake.

The lamp did not appear to be in the area Rhyn had advised her to search, so she moved around, wondering if it had been nudged about by the water. She began to worry that it was not there after all when she noticed a glint coming from among the seaweed on the lake's floor. Floating over to it, she filled with excitement as she saw that it was, in fact, the lamp. Now if only she could move it.

The magic pulse was as strong as ever, and she tapped into it as she focused on the lamp, willing it to become untangled from the seaweed. It shifted, but remained stuck within its grasp. She changed her attention to the seaweed and tried to move it out of the way. Again, they shifted but did not move completely apart. As frustration grew within her, she could feel the magic changing. She watched as the seaweed around the lamp withered away until it disintegrated. And then so did all the seaweed around it for several feet. At least the lamp was free now.

Turning her attention back to it, she again

willed it move, and this time it shot through the water and erupted out of the lake's surface. Enya darted up to the surface, seeing Nole and Rhyn had turned at the sound. Unfortunately, she was also not entirely certain how to speak while in this form so she eased her way up the side of the lake where her clothes were with a mental huff. As she flowed onto the land, her shape began to return.

"Turn around," she called as soon as she could.

The men did so. Once her physical form was completely restored, the sword flew back into her hand. She set it at her feet, which it seemed to find acceptable, and yanked on her clothes.

"All right, I'm decent."

"Did you find it?" Rhyn asked as he turned back.

"Yes, but my magic made it shoot out of the water."

"I thought that's what that was," Nole said.

"Did you see where it landed?"

"Over there." Rhyn started to lead the way.

"Any ideas how to get this blasted sword to leave me be?" Enya said as it flew to her once more when she started walking.

"Hold on." Rhyn waved his hand and a sheath zoomed at them from several feet away. "Here, let me help you strap it on."

She sheathed the sword and he instructed her on how to strap it to her back, since he could not touch it himself, explaining the best way for it to be easily drawn.

"I doubt that will be an issue."

Once it was in place, they continued on and came upon the lamp, glistening in the moonlight amongst the grass.

Enya bent over it and took it up in her hands. "Well, this is it then. I can't believe it was actually here, but it is. Now we can get Jack back."

She rubbed the side of the lamp and green smoke poured out of it, growing until it became the shape of a woman with green skin, a long black ponytail, silken clothes, and golden bangles on her arms. Below her waist, she trailed off into smoke that still connected to the lamp. She observed the three standing before her and turned her attention to Enya.

"You get three wishes." She crossed her arms, and her voice sounded a bit bored.

"Can't raise anyone from the dead or wish for more wishes. What is your first wish?

"I wish for my brother Jack to be brought here," Enya said.

The djinn waved a hand and green smoke flooded from it, billowing out to a size a little larger than Enya and swirling and thickening until it started to solidify. Then the smoke faded away to leave a figure blinking in confusion facing them. Enya's jaw dropped.

"You're not Jack."

6 - What's Really Going On

"*WHAT HAVE YOU* done with me?" the young satyr demanded. "Who are you? Take me back!"

"Well this was unexpected," Nole said, looking over the newcomer. He had a similar build to Rhyn, but his disheveled hair was blue and had a texture more like seaweed, similar to Enya's, and he was much younger and more vibrant than the older satyr. He wore velvet pajamas under a silken robe.

"Who are you?" Enya asked.

The satyr straightened up. "I'm Xorphiul, prince of elves, and I demand you take me back to the palace."

"Elves?" Nole turned to Enya. "Wasn't Jack rather elfish?"

"Hm." Enya tilted her head in consideration. "You're a satyr... And you came when I wished for my brother..."

"He must be your real brother then," Rhyn concluded.

"What are you talking about?" Xorphiul asked.

"Clearly Jack was a changeling[27]," Rhyn explained. "They must have switched the two of you when you were babies. He's the real Xorphiul and you're the real Jack."

"That would certainly explain a lot," Enya said. "Though it does us no good in finding Jack. My Jack, I mean."

"Let me get this straight," Nole said. "You were looking for your brother, only he wasn't really your brother, and now you have another brother, who's here now, but your brother, whom you thought was your real brother, isn't?"

"I think so," Enya said with a frown. "You're making my head hurt." She put her fingers to her temple and groaned. "I just wish I knew what was really going on."

"No, don't—" Rhyn started, but it was too late. Smoke poured from the djinn and covered his face. "I was the one who hired Nole to kidnap Jack."

Enya gawked at him. His eyes were

---

[27] elf child left in exchange for the child of another; it is considered very rude, but no one can find the elves to complain

clouded with green smoke. "You did *what*? Why would you do that?"

"Because I knew he couldn't be your real brother, so I thought if I could get you to wish for your brother, the djinn would undoubtedly bring your real twin instead."

"Wait, are you telling me that this whole thing was one big fabrication just to get me to the lamp?" Enya put her hands on her hips.

"Yes. It was the only way to find him, aside from tracking down the elves and exploring all of their lands, which would take far too much time, and they usually don't reveal themselves to outsiders anyway."

"What do you want with me?" Xorphiul asked.

"I need both of you in order to complete the spell," Rhyn said.

"What spell?" Enya asked.

"It will revive all the old Maven and force them to fight for us. Only nobility can be used to trigger it, and you two are the closest things we have to nobility amongst the Maven. Together, we will bring the lands under the Union once more and Thero will rule us all, as he should."

"Who's Thero?"

"The great and powerful lord of the Union."

"If you knew where the lamp was, why didn't you just make the wish yourself?" Enya could feel her anger stirring up her magic. It prickled through her chest and arms.

"I already used up all of my wishes during the final battle."

Enya gasped. "You were the satyr whose wish caused all the deaths!"

"Some of them. And it was accidental."

"Like that matters! You still lied to us about literally everything!" She threw her arm out to emphasize her words, and a blast of energy slammed into everyone around her, knocking them to the ground. She vaguely regretted that Nole and Xorphiul had gotten caught up in it, but her rage at Rhyn quickly overtook all other thoughts. She stormed toward him.

"Maybe if you had just explained everything in the first place, I would have made the wish anyway! Did you ever consider that? But now Jack has been who-knows-where for days!"

"He's safe, with the Black Matron," Rhyn said. She could see him struggling to control his words, but the green smoke still covered his eyes.

"The Black Matron? Of *Death*? How could he possibly be safe there?" Enya shouted.

Before Rhyn could answer, the ground around him erupted into flames, causing Enya to gasp and look down at her arms. She had felt the magic leave her, but now she could not think what to do about it. She reached out to try to quench it with magic, but it just spread further.

Rhyn sprung out of the midst of it and made a dash for the lake. Thrusting a hand out toward it, the surface swirled and turned into a portal, which he leapt through and was gone.

"Wait!" Enya cried, but it was too late. She looked back at the flames, which caught on the grass all around, plunging them into a wildfire.

"Put it out!" Nole cried.

"I can't!" Enya called back.

Xorphiul jumped into the lake.

"Good idea," Nole said, running to follow. "Enya, come on."

She grimaced at the thought of turning into water again, wondering if her clothes would even survive the fire by the time she was able to emerge. She tugged on the magic within her, trying one last time to put out the flames, but she wasn't sure what she was doing. Her eyes darted to the lake and she willed it to wash over the land and drench it. It surged at her influence and she realized at the last minute that not only would she be turned to liquid this way anyway, but Nole and Xorphiul would be thrown from the pool along with the water. Already it built into a giant wave, looming over her. She put a hand out to stop it, but it grew even taller, pulling all the water in the lake into the tidal wave. Then she remembered the lamp in her other hand.

"I wish I had control over magic!"

Just before the wave came crashing down on her, she found herself surrounded by green smoke. And then she was floating along the bank with the current as it doused the flames. The djinn was no longer visible. She heard Xorphiul and Nole sputtering and skimmed along toward them.

"Are you all right?" she called to them, only she was in her liquid state and could not speak.

"I think so," Nole said between coughs, pushing himself to his knees. The water around him was now about a half-foot high and quickly diminishing as it spread along the ground, the glow it once carried growing dimmer every second.

"*Wait, did you hear me?*" she asked.

"Um," he looked around for her, "I think so. Or, somehow."

The water continued to drain, and Enya's shape began returning. For a moment she panicked as she realized she must have lost her clothes somewhere, but as she felt her skin materialize, she saw that the clothes and sword had come with her this time, though the lamp was no longer clutched in her hand.

"Thank gods for that wish," she said, checking in on the energy pulse. It was still strong, but now she could create the funnel around it with no effort at all. She turned her attention to Xorphiul and approached him. "What about you? You all right?"

"I seem to be," he said. "Though I'm very confused."

"I don't blame you."

He pushed himself to his hooves and sighed. "So, I'm not really an elf then?"

Enya raised an eyebrow. "Did you really think you were?"

"Of course I did." Xorphiul frowned at her. "Everyone told me I was."

"So the fact that you were twice their size with goat legs and blue hair didn't give you a hint that you might be something else?"

"I guess I never really thought about it."

She shook her head. "I always knew Jack wasn't a satyr, even though everyone always told us we were twins."

"Then why were you so adamant about finding him?" Nole asked.

She glared at him. "He's still a brother to me. We were raised together for eighteen years. I can't just leave him to die."

"I'm guessing I'm not a prince, either then," Xorphiul said mournfully.

"Not exactly."

"Where are you from?"

"A gnome farm."

"A *farm?* I'm not going to live on a *farm.*"

Enya crossed her arms. "It happens to be a wonderful place to live. But you don't have to live there. You can go back to your elf land if you want."

"I would prefer that," he said, rubbing his neck. "But will they take me back if they know I'm not an elf?"

"They're the ones who switched you in the

first place!"

"Oh, right."

"So, what exactly is the plan now?" Nole said, wringing water from his cloak.

"I still need to save Jack. So I guess we have to find the Black Matron."

"You're actually going to go looking for the Black Matron?" Xorphiul looked at her as though she had three heads.

"I have to. Besides, now I have control over my magic, so there shouldn't be much danger."

"And what about me?" The satyr's tail swished. "I suppose I'm to be left to wander about all on my own."

"Gods, aren't you melodramatic," Enya said. "I'm not going to just leave you to rot. You're my brother too, apparently, so I'll see you to safety once we've rescued Jack."

"Actually, we could probably see him to safety before we've rescued Jack," Nole said. "That is, if everything is where I think they are."

"What do you mean?"

"Rumor has it the Black Matron is stationed in the old castle of Qinar. Rumor also has it that the elves live somewhere in the forests of Chun. Right?" he addressed

Xorphiul.

"I'm not really supposed to tell others that..."

"Then how are we to get you back?" Enya snapped.

"Good point. Yes, Chun."

"Chun is in between here and Qinar," Nole continued. "We can drop him off along the way. Actually, it's not all that far, even. If Rhyn had just known that, he probably could have found him on his own."

"He never would have found me there," Xorphiul said, rising in stature again. "We're not found unless we wish to be."

"Or are wished to be, apparently," Nole chuckled. Xorphiul glared at him. "OMD[28], you two are definitely related."

"I'm assuming they'll let us find them because you'll be with us?" Enya asked.

"Of course."

"Then I guess that's our next destination." She eyed the sky. "It's almost morning, so we'll stay here until tonight."

"Tonight?" Xorphiul crinkled his forehead.

"Vampire," Nole said, pointing to himself.

––––––––

[28] a slang term that utilizes the Lord Dracula's name to express surprise or sarcasm

"Oh, right."

He sat down on the ground and tossed his still dripping cloak into the air, letting it float down to cover him.

"What's he doing?" Xorphiul asked.

"Protecting himself from the sun." She sat down as well and motioned for Xorphiul to do the same. "So, Xorphiul. Tell me about yourself."

"I already did." He sat near her. "I'm the elf prince."

"Besides that."

He shrugged. "I don't know how to answer that."

Enya didn't know how to clarify, so they sat in silence for a moment.

"I never had a sister before," Xorphiul said finally. "Or any siblings for that matter."

"There, that's something. So you thought you were an only child. What's that like?"

"I don't know; pretty boring, I guess." He tilted his head. "I just realized, I never caught your name."

"Enya. And that's Nole," she pointed to the black cloak.

"Are you a naiad?"

"I am."

"I thought they were all dead. Satyrs, too."

"Obviously some survived."

They fell silent again.

"Well, great talk," Enya said. "I'm going to get some rest now. You should, too."

"But I just got up for the day. You know, because I live by days like normal people."

"At least try to nap or something later then." She lay down and tugged her cloak tight around her. It occurred to her that it was dry. The magic she had used to bring it with her when she transformed must have protected it from the water. In a way, despite the unexpected betrayal from Rhyn, things were actually looking up. She now had a decent idea where Jack was, as well as the truth behind the whole twin thing she had always wondered about, and she could control her magic now. All things considered, it had been a productive night.

She soon drifted off to sleep, but Xorphiul could not. As he tried to sort out all the strange things that had just happened, his thoughts mulled over the djinn and the lamp Enya had been holding before the wave. He wondered what had happened to it. A djinn's lamp was legendary, and this may be the only chance he had to find one.

He ventured around the area until he saw

the sunlight reflecting off of gold. He picked up the lamp and looked it over, trying to think of a good wish. Supposing he could wish himself back home, he made to rub the lamp, but stopped. The others had already agreed to take him there, and the vampire had said they weren't far. Why waste a wish on something he was going to easily get anyway?

As hard as he thought, however, he could not come up with anything else urgent enough at the moment, so he decided to save the wishes until they were needed. Attaching the lamp to his cord belt, he pulled his robe closed over it and tied it in place.

♦

As Rhyn fell through the portal, gravity shifted and he found himself parallel to the floor, onto which he soon crashed. The portal closed behind him and he rubbed his back as he rose.

"Did you find him?" the voice rang through his mind.

Rhyn turned to see the Black Matron facing him. "Yes, but things went south as soon as I did. I had to flee."

"He will not be pleased."

"There is still a chance. I told them the boy was with you, and Enya is determined to rescue him. I didn't get the chance to tell them where the castle is, but with any luck they'll have heard the rumors and come here to us. And there is one other thing."

The Black Matron waited for more.

"The boy is not just any boy. He's the prince of the elves. I think now would be a good time to test out that spell."

"He wanted us to use it on the Maven."

"We can do both. This will just be an added bonus. Now get it ready. We're doing this tonight."

7 - The Elf Kingdom

THAT NIGHT, ENYA realized they were going to have more trouble than she expected when Xorphiul backed away from Rhyn's pegasus.

"You expect me to ride *that?*"

"You've never ridden one before, have you?"

"Certainly not."

She considered this. "You might be able to ride with me on mine, but we'd probably be too heavy to fly very fast..."

"Can't you just use magic to help him along?" Nole suggested.

"I don't really know. Rhyn only taught me a few things. But I suppose I could try." She turned to Xorphiul. "I'll help you mount, and then just leave the rest to me."

He frowned at her but did as she said, nearly toppling off when she boosted him up. Enya waved a hand over the pegasus while directing her intentions, and a barrier covered Xorphiul and the pegasus.

"Now you shouldn't be able to fall off," she said, hoping it was true.

Xorphiul shifted around a little to test. "Yes, I do seem to be prevented from that."

"Good," Enya said with a sigh of relief. "Now, if your pegasus ever starts to buck, I'll try to calm it with magic." She shook her head. "Listen to me, talking like a sorceress. Last week I wanted nothing to do with magic. Still don't, but what can you do?"

They left for Chun, and Xorphiul squeezed his eyes shut much of the way.

"You don't have to worry about falling," Enya reminded him.

"If I look down, I'll vomit," Xorphiul said.

"Fair enough."

After some time, Nole spoke up. "We should be in the area now, so I do actually need you to look so you can tell us where is best to land."

Xorphiul took in a deep breath and opened his eyes in a squint. He peered down at the tops of the trees for a second before closing his eyes again, holding back a gag. "I'm not sure, it all looks different from up here."

"We'll just land and walk," Enya said. She helped guide Xorphiul's pegasus to the ground with her magic while she and Nole landed beside him. "Anything look familiar?"

Xorphiul looked around. "Yes, but we're about an hour from the castle."

"How can you even tell?" Enya asked. "It all looks the same."

He shrugged. "I've spent my whole life out here. I know it like the back of my hand."

With Xorphiul in the lead, the trio and the pegasi made their way through the forest on foot.

"We aren't going to have to stop just before we reach it, are we?" Enya asked Nole, noticing dawn was building.

"I should be fine so long as I'm hidden by the trees or inside the castle."

"We're here," Xorphiul announced, coming to a stop.

The others looked around.

"We are?" Enya couldn't see anything remotely resembling a castle.

"I do smell others nearby," Nole said as he sniffed, "but I don't see anyone."

"Mom! Dad! I'm home!" Xorphiul cried, striding forward.

The large oak tree in front of them creaked and groaned as a knot opened up into a small entranceway. Xorphiul motioned the others to follow as he began to step inside.

"Actually, I'm going to need a verbal welcome in order to enter," Nole said.

"Oh, right. You may come in."

Nole followed the satyr while Enya tied the pegasi to a nearby tree and hurried after them before the knot closed. They went down a stairway to a spacious underground hallway. The glowing lights along the ceiling illuminated intricate designs along the walls and roof, made of firmly packed soil.

"This looks sturdy," Nole said, eyeing their surroundings.

"It's stabilized with fairy[29] magic," Xorphiul assured him.

"Xorphiul, you're back!" an older elf cried, hobbling to greet him. He paused when he noticed the other two with him. "Who are they?"

"They helped me find my way home," Xorphiul explained.

"That's a vampire."

He glanced at Nole. "Yes."

"You gave a vampire permission to enter

---

[29] little glowing insect-like spirits that are made almost entirely of magic and jealousy

our castle."

"Well, yes. But like I said, he helped me get here. And this," he pointed to Enya, "is apparently my sister."

She waved. "Hello."

"Ah." The elf's face grew more serious. "So then..."

"I know I'm not an elf." Xorphiul hunched his shoulders in remorse.

"Xorphiul!" a woman's voice called out, and another elf came to them. She, too, paused at the sight of the newcomers.

"He knows," the elf man said.

"Oh. Well, we had best discuss this over breakfast then."

As they headed for the eating hall, Xorphiul made introductions.

"Mom, Dad, this is Enya and Nole. Enya, Nole, this is my mom and dad, the king and queen of the elves."

Nole bowed as best he could while walking. "Your Majesties."

"Nice to meet you," Enya said, only bowing her head.

The king and queen gave small, forced smiles. They all entered the dining hall. It was rather small, with only one long table in the middle.

"Not exactly what I'd expect from a castle," Nole murmured under his breath.

The king clapped his hands and summoned a younger elf.

"Go fetch us all breakfast," he ordered.

The elf eyed the group before hurrying off to obey. They settled down in their chairs, with the king at the head of the table, the queen to his right, and Xorphiul to his left. Enya and Nole sat on Xorphiul's side. The elf returned within seconds with a platter almost as big as he and set it down on the table, and then lifted the lid to reveal several small dishes of odd looking but delicious smelling food. Another elf followed with dishes, which she laid out before each of them. Xorphiul dug right in, and Enya did so as well at his encouragement. The king and queen took small amounts, and Nole politely declined anything.

"Now then," the king said to Xorphiul once they had all served up. "How much do you know?"

"I know that Enya is my sister," he said around a mouthful of food. Swallowing, he continued. "And I know I'm really a satyr. Also, there's an elf named Jack who was raised as Enya's brother who's been kidnapped."

"He's been kidnapped?" The queen sat forward with alarm and exchanged a look with her husband.

"Blarn," the king cursed, "we still didn't stop it!"

"Stop what?" Xorphiul said, pausing with his fork halfway to his mouth.

His so-called parents exchanged another glance before the king answered. "There was a prophecy that the elf prince would be stolen away. That's why we switched the two of you. We thought he would be safe as long as you were given the title of 'elf prince.'"

Xorphiul frowned. "How would that help?"

"They were using you as bait," Enya explained, shoving her plate away. "They wanted you to be stolen away instead."

"Which did happen," the queen pointed out.

"Only because Jack was stolen away first," Enya said. "I never would have accidentally wished Xorphiul away from here if I wasn't trying to find Jack."

"And Jack never would have been stolen away if Rhyn hadn't known there was a switch and tricked Enya into making the wish in the first place," Nole said. "So really, you brought this all on yourself."

"Oh," the king said, his cheeks turning a bit pink.

"So... Are you telling me you never actually cared about me?" Xorphiul had finally found his voice after Enya's revelation, though there was a catch in it. "You were just using me because you thought it would protect Jack?"

When the elves did not answer, Xorphiul found it to be answer enough. He stood, knocking his chair over. "In that case, it seems I'm no longer welcome here. Enya, Nole, let's get out of here."

Enya rose and put her hands on the table. "You know, I could tell Jack wasn't my real brother since I was little, but I loved him anyway. That's why I'm still trying to save him. How could you raise Xorphiul from a baby and not care about him at all?"

"We didn't say that," the queen said. "We do care, and we were concerned when he disappeared, but he's not our son."

"You're the ones who stole him away from his guardians in the first place, so you have no right to treat him like an outsider now." Enya's scowl deepened. "Why didn't you just hide Jack away and leave Xorphiul be? Then no one would have been considered the elf prince, and maybe no one would have been stolen away."

"We had to take Xorphiul," the king explained. "It would have been suspicious if there was an extra baby there."

Enya's gawked. "Right, because gods forbid the exchange of an elf and a satyr be obvious." She shook her head. "You two are ridiculous."

"How dare you!" the king cried, jumping to his feet. "We are the great royal majesties of the elf kingdom!"

"I don't give a jackalope's ass," Enya said. "You can't do that to someone. He would have been perfectly content if he had just stayed with me and was raised by the gnomes, but now he lived his whole life with the expectation that he'd be a prince, with the belief that he had a pair of loving parents, and then you just ripped that away from him. It's cruel!"

"Um, Enya?" Nole said.

"What?" she snapped.

"I think we should get out of here." He sniffed the air. "Something really isn't right."

"What are you talking about?"

"I'm not sure, but I'm smelling blood and

some sort of rot, and I think I can hear screams in the distance."

"Screams?" the queen echoed, straining to hear for herself.

"Yes, definitely screams," Nole confirmed. "And they're coming this way."

He turned and made for the hallway before halting. "The rotting smell is that way, too."

"What is it?" Enya asked.

"I have no idea."

"Is there another way out?" she asked Xorphiul.

He nodded, fighting back tears, and started for a different hallway to the left.

"That one, too," Nole said. "It's all around us now."

"Then it doesn't matter," Enya said. "Let's just pick one and go with it."

The three of them went down the left hallway, and the king and queen ran to follow.

"You can't be serious," Enya said when she noticed.

"You expect us to just sit around and wait for whatever is coming to attack us?" the king said.

"It's what you deserve." Enya sighed. "But

you're Jack's parents too, so I guess I have to help you."

"Holy minotaur[30]!" Nole cried, pointing ahead.

Four of what could only be considered elves stumbled toward them, but they did not look like the other elves they had seen. Their skin was dirty and discolored, and part of it had come off in chunks. They wore clothes that appeared to have once been very nice, but now were tattered and dirt-stained. As they closed in on the group, they reached out for them, groaning unintelligibly. The sword flew into Enya's hand.

"What in all the gods names are those?" she shouted.

"I think they're dead," Nole said. "Or, were."

"But they're moving!" Xorphiul said.

"Astute observation," Nole confirmed.

"You said they are coming from every direction?" Enya glanced over her shoulder and thought she saw something moving at the end of the hallway where they had come from.

---

[30] bull's upper body with man's legs, not to be confused with an ophiotaurus, which has no legs

"Afraid so."

"Then I guess we'll have to make do with this route." Ignoring the sword, Enya punched out toward the zombie elves and sent a shockwave at them. "Hurry, let's get out of here before they get up."

They ran through the hallway, stepping over the moaning figures as they did. Just when they thought they were clear, the king screamed. Enya turned back to see his ankle had been grabbed by one of the undead. With a huff, she directed her magic to move the ground around its arm, pinning it down. It growled and lunged its upper body forward, biting the king's calf and causing him to cry out again. Enya looked to the ceiling, and at her nudge the soil roof above the undead collapsed. The momentum pushed the one clutching the king away while the queen darted over to him and grabbed his arm, tugging him forward.

"Are you all right?" she asked.

"My leg!" he gasped.

Blood gushed from the wound, and Nole inched back, subconsciously licking his lips.

"We need to get out of here," Enya said.

They hurried through the rest of the hallway, coming to an exit that led out another large tree. Nole hesitated at the opening.

"Is there heavy shade nearby?"

"Over there." Enya pointed. "Put your cloak up."

He did so and she pulled him along to the shadiest spot she could find while the others scrambled after them. The queen eased the king onto the ground, his breathing labored and sweat coating his forehead.

"He doesn't smell so good," Nole cautioned. "I think that thing gave him an infection."

"It happened two minutes ago," the queen snapped. "How could he already have an infection?"

"I'm just telling you what it smells like," Nole said, holding up his hands.

"Let me see the bite," Enya said. She crouched over the small figure, gently twisting his leg to see for herself. It was green and filled with pus beneath his pant leg where it had been ripped open by the undead's teeth.

"Enya, get away from him," Nole said. "His blood is spreading the taint throughout his body."

No sooner did he speak than the king

lunged at her, gnashing his teeth. She pulled away just in time.

"Get to the pegasi," Nole cried. "There's more coming. We have to get out of here."

Sure enough, several more undead elves came into view, stumbling through the forest toward them.

"But what about you?" she said. "You can't fly in daylight."

"Good point. I can probably run through the forest, as long as I keep to the shade and hold my cloak over me."

"Then we'll stick to the ground," Enya said.

She started for the pegasi but Nole held up an arm to stop her.

"Actually, they seem to be eating the pegasi. Let's just run. That way is clearest."

They turned in the direction he indicated.

"We can't just leave him!" the queen cried.

"He's one of them now," Enya said. "There's nothing we can do about that, except make sure we don't become one, too."

But her words came too late, for Nole cried out as the king, whom they had stopped watching too closely, jumped at him and bit him on the arm. Enya grabbed the elf by the throat and he released his grip, so she threw him to the side. He skidded along the ground a few feet.

"Does this mean you're going to change, too?" she asked the vampire who clutched at the wound on his arm.

"Probably. But I can at least help you get away before it takes over," he said through clenched teeth. "When I feel it start to change me, I'll head the other way, but until then I'll direct you out of here."

Enya nodded with a frown and they all ran off through the trees. The queen did not.

"Mom?" Xorphiul called back to her when he noticed.

"I can't leave him," she said, tears dripping down her cheeks. She flinched as her husband tackled her, biting her on the shoulder.

"Mom!"

"She's not your mother," Enya said. "And it's too late now. Let's get out of here while we still can."

They dashed through the woods, Nole following his nose to get them through in the safest manner while shielding himself with the cloak.

"I think we're out of danger," he said after a few minutes. "They all are focused on the castle for now."

"How's your arm?" Enya asked.

Nole pulled back his sleeve to check. "Hm, it doesn't look any worse than it did at first."

She checked it herself. "It's not gross at all. And it's been much longer than the king's."

"How is that possible?" Nole asked. "When the werewolf bit me, I was infected that night." He pulled his sleeve up further to show another bite, this one long healed over into a nasty scar.

"Maybe this one only effects elves," Enya said. It was the only explanation she could think of. "And you really need to stop letting yourself get bitten by monsters."

"He wasn't a monster," Xorphiul said mournfully. "Or maybe he was. I don't know anymore."

Enya put a hand on his shoulder. Normally she avoided physical contact, but he looked as though he could use some right now.

"I'm sorry they did that. You deserved better. But it's beyond our control. You're welcome to stick with us if you'd like. We are family, after all. Real family."

He nodded as a tear slipped from his eye

and he wiped it away. "Thank you."

"We should probably move a little more before stopping for the day," Nole said. "They could always change their minds about who they feel like attacking."

Trudging along for a bit longer, Nole started yawning.

"The infection may not have taken you, but you look like you could do with some sleep," Enya said after the seventh yawn.

He nodded. "I think we should be all right here for now."

"I'll keep watch just in case," Enya said.

The men hunkered down and Xorphiul tugged his robe tightly around him.

"What will you do when you find Jack?" he asked.

"What do you mean?"

"You said you still think of him as a brother. So what happens to me when you find him?"

She shrugged. "We'll all go back to the farm. It's not like I can't have more than one brother. And he doesn't exactly have anywhere else to go now, either."

Xorphiul nodded sadly and dozed off fitfully. He awoke an hour later when he rolled on his side and felt a hard lump.

Feeling around, he realized it was the lamp. With all the commotion he had forgotten about it.

He bolted upright. The lamp! He could wish for the elves to be restored! Freeing it from his belt—and regretting he had not had the chance to change out of his pajamas—he put his hand on the side...

Only...

They *had* been lying to him his whole life. And it was clear they did not actually care about him. As far as they were concerned, he was merely bait.

He pulled his hand away. They deserved this. They were heartless, manipulative beings who cared for no one but themselves. Let them rot.

Tears sprung up in his eyes once more and he did not fight them this time. It wasn't fair. They were supposed to be his family. Enya clearly still considered Jack family even though she had known the whole time.

Xorphiul looked at his sister, who had dozed off at her post. Sister. This was his real family, not those fakes. She had stood up for him at breakfast, so she must care about him already. Maybe she would soon love him as much as she loved Jack.

Jack. Xorphiul had the lamp. He could wish Jack here. Enya would be so pleased. For the third time since he'd gotten it, Xorphiul reached to rub the lamp, and for the third time he stopped.

Enya loved Jack so much she was willing to face the Black Matron herself just to save him. They had spent eighteen years together, but she had only known him for one day. If Jack came back now, he'd take all of her attention. She might even forget about Xorphiul. No, he needed to bond with her first before Jack stole the spotlight. That old satyr did say he was safe, so what would a few more days matter? He could always use his wish to help them when they reached the castle if things got dangerous. Until then, he would keep the lamp hidden and do whatever he could to win his sister's loyalty.

8 - Resistance

IT WAS SLOW going without the pegasi. Nole still showed no signs of infection, and his arm was healing up rather swiftly.

"At least that's something," Enya said.

"Vampires heal faster than some other creatures," Nole explained. "It should take us a few extra nights to get to the headquarters."

"I just hope Jack will still be there when we get there. They might decide they don't need him anymore."

"Are you kidding? Rhyn wants the two of you. Of course he'd keep Jack where he knows you know to look."

"Which means that he'll be waiting for us." Enya huffed.

"We'll just have to be extra careful. He may be a Maven, but you have way more magic than he does, and you can control it now."

"Not to mention this handy sword." Enya

rolled her eyes. "As if I knew what to do with it."

Nole stopped walking.

"What is it now?" Enya moaned.

"We're going to make a pit stop on the way to Qinar."

"What? Why? You just said we're already going to be running behind. Not to mention what happened the last time we made a detour."

"Trust me, you'll want this one." He ran a hand through his hair. "I've been debating about it because, well, they sort of disbanded... But I think, given the circumstances, we could try to regroup."

"Just get to the point."

"I know where her headquarters is because I used to be involved with a group that was dedicated to finding and defeating her. I never actually encountered her myself, but they did narrow down her location before she obliterated half of the group."

"Obliterated?" Xorphiul squeaked.

"She didn't get her name for no reason," Nole said. "Anyway, that's why they disbanded. They decided she was too much of a threat for us in our current state and she wasn't really doing much at the time unless provoked, so they just left her be. But I'm sure some of the remainders are still around. Some of them know sword fighting, and they would have more information about her than I do."

"If you were part of this group, why don't you know those things?"

"I wasn't really interested in all that."

"Then why were you a part of the group in the first place?"

He looked away. "I was trying to impress someone. But I was too much of a coward to actually get involved with the resistance part."

"It sounds to me like that was the entire point."

"It was."

"So you basically did nothing."

"Pretty much."

She shook her head. "I'm guessing she wasn't too impressed, then."

"It wasn't a she. And no, he wasn't."

Enya's eyes widened. "Oh. So that's why I'm not your type."

Nole shrugged. His face was more somber than usual.

"What happened to him?" she asked.

"He was amongst those obliterated."

"Sorry to hear that."

He sighed. "It was a long time ago."

"Still."

Xorphiul had been quiet this whole time, but he became intrigued as he listened to the story. "How did you handle it?"

"I took off. Moved to Cromsen. Tried to forget."

"Did it work?"

Nole said nothing.

"Are you sure you won't mind trying to bring the resistance back together?" Enya asked.

"Does that really matter? It's our best chance at surviving. Something I happen to care about very much."

"Well, thank you then."

He shrugged again.

It took three more nights for them to arrive at Sirio, a town even seedier than Cromsen, which Enya did not know was possible. Nole headed straight for a small run-down shack and pounded on the door. After a moment, it inched open.

"Nole? Is that you?" The door opened

wider to reveal a sleepy ogre[31].

"Yes, it's me."

"Come in," the ogre said, allowing the three inside. "I see you have new friends."

"These are Enya and Xorphiul." He gestured to the ogre. "And this is Gsuzat."

"Incredible," Gsuzat breathed. "You found both a satyr and a naiad?"

"It's a long story."

"Come, sit down, and I'll make you two a spot of tea. Nole, I could let you have one of my cockatrices[32]."

"That is so generous of you," Nole said, bowing his head.

They made themselves comfortable on the couch while Gsuzat stepped out of the room for a few moments, coming back with a tray holding three cups of tea in one hand and another tray holding a freshly dead cockatrice in the other. They all thanked him as they received their respective refreshments.

"What brings you back?" Gsuzat asked Nole, blowing over his steaming cup before

---

[31] monstrous polite beast

[32] small roosters or chickens with the legs of a dragon and the temperament of a Chihuahua

taking a sip.

"We need to reinstate the Resistance."

Gsuzat choked on his tea. "You are the last person I would expect to hear that from."

"My brother is being held captive by the Black Matron," Enya explained.

"I hate to break it to you, but he's probably long dead by now if that's the case."

She shook her head. "They want me to come after him. They need me and Xorphiul for some sort of spell. But if they succeed, they'll revive the Maven and try to take over everything, so we have to get Jack back without getting caught."

"Jack? What a strange name."

"You're missing the point." Enya's eyes flashed.

"Calm down," Nole soothed with his old sweetness dripping from his words. He turned his attention back to Gsuzat. "She's determined to save him, so I thought the best course of action would be to gather the Resistance once more, teach her a thing or two about using her sword, and work together to get Jack out of there without them being captured themselves."

"I don't know." Gsuzat tapped his heel on the floor, jostling his leg. "You saw what happened the last time we tried to stop her. And there's less of us now than there were then. This is a high order for just one boy, especially considering the risk if we fail."

"So you're just not going to help at all?" Enya said.

Gsuzat sighed. "I'm afraid not."

"Well, this was a waste of time." She stood and put her teacup down on the table. "Thanks for the tea."

"You can at least stay here for the day, if you'd like," Gsuzat said. "I just can't do anything about the Resistance."

"Enya, we should stay," Nole said. "It'll be hard to find another place that'll take in a vampire at this time of day."

"Fine."

"I'll make up the guest room." Gsuzat stood and left.

"You could be a little nicer," Nole said. "He is a friend of mine."

"But now we're back to square one." Enya paced the room. "So we're just going to have to storm the castle on our own after all. This was so pointless."

"At least it didn't delay us, really," Nole

said. "And now we have an actual place to sleep for the day."

"I guess."

"That does sound nice," Xorphiul said, twisting his cup in his hands.

"We'll rest for now and head out tonight, like normal. And just hope that your magic will be enough to work on its own."

Gsuzat returned and showed them to the guest room, which featured three cots, each with a set of sheets.

"I'm sorry I can't be of more help," he said.

"This will do," Nole assured him, ignoring Enya's mutters.

They each picked a cot and settled down for the night.

"What the blazes?" Enya shouted as she woke to find herself bound with magic and being tossed over Gsuzat's shoulder.

"Gsuzat!" Nole struggled against his own bounds while the ogre tossed Xorphiul over his other shoulder.

"I really am sorry about this, Nole, but I have no choice. It's mayhem out there, and the other satyr said he'd spare anyone who turned in the twins."

"You're just going to hand us over?" Enya twisted around, trying to wriggle out of his grasp, but the magic held her in place. "You give us tea and a place to sleep and then you just give us to them?"

"It was not my intention when you first arrived, but the zombie[33] elves are killing everyone. I have to do something. This is the only way to stop it."

Enya grunted while Gsuzat strode through the house to the front door. She nudged at the restraints with her own magic. It sliced through it like butter, and she pushed off of the ogre, slipping from his grasp. Gsuzat paused to try to reclaim her, but she repeated the process on Xorphiul and he was soon free as well.

"That's not possible!" Gsuzat cried, reaching out a hand toward Enya. She felt the magic beginning to constrict her once more, but she fought it back and willed for the same barrier around Gsuzat that she had used to keep Xorphiul from falling off the pegasus, only tighter. Now it was the ogre's turn to struggle to no avail, stuck where he stood.

---

[33] undead beings revived and controlled through magic

"Let's get out of here," she called to her brother and darted back to the guest room to free Nole.

"I swear I had no idea he would do that." Nole hopped up as soon as he was released.

"We had better get out of the city," Enya said.

"But the sun hasn't set yet." Xorphiul gestured to the window, where there was still a hint of light coming from behind the heavy curtain.

"There's a sewer nearby," Nole said. "I think I can reach it if I'm careful." He sniffed a few times. "We better hurry though, because I think the zombie elves are heading this direction."

They didn't need to be told twice. Running past the ogre, who yelled at them from his entrapment, the trio made for the door and huddled together with Nole in the middle, sticking close to the sides of the buildings until they reached the sewer grate two doors down. As soon as Enya bent and yanked it open, Nole jumped inside.

Enya grabbed the sides and lowered herself so she was hanging. "Blast."

"What?" Xorphiul called down to her, glancing up as he heard the screams getting closer.

"This whole thing is holding sewage water. I'll be transformed as soon as I touch it. There's no way I'm floating around in *that*."

"We don't exactly have any other options." Xorphiul's voice was urgent. The zombies had come into his view.

"Just drop," Nole shouted.

Enya huffed, closed her eyes, and let go, but instead of splashing into the water, Nole caught her in his arms.

"Xor, come on," he called.

Xorphiul swung down, pulling the grate across the top before dropping the rest of the way. Nole turned away in time to shield Enya from the splash.

"Where do we go from here?" the satyr asked, trying not to think about what he was standing in.

"I know a place where we should be safe from the zombies."

"Can we reach it from the sewers?"

Nole nodded. "Yes, but it's on the other side of town, so we'll be in here for a while."

"Sounds pleasant," Enya said.

"We're the ones who have to run through it," Nole said. "I can always drop you."

"And I can always blast you to bits."

Nole rolled his eyes. "Not even a thank you for saving you from a nauseating fate."

"Thank you for saving me from a nauseating fate," Enya echoed.

"See? Being civil never hurt anyone."

"I don't know," Enya said. "Gsuzat was pretty civil and he nearly hurt us."

"I stand corrected." He stiffened. "Oh blazes."

"What?" Enya asked.

"It just dawned on me that we left him bound by magic in the middle of a city being terrorized by zombie elves."

"Oh. I hadn't really thought about that at the time," Enya admitted.

"Maybe the barrier around him will also prevent the elves from being able to touch him. He may have betrayed us, but he used to be my friend, and I certainly do not wish death upon him. He was just doing what he thought would save the city."

"Can we just get out of here?" Xorphiul whined.

"Right," Nole said and took off to the right.

Xorphiul followed. "You seem to know these pretty well."

"I sometimes took this route to get to the Resistance's meeting hall. Good news about sewers is they offer shade without needing permission to enter."

"What happens when you try to enter someplace without permission?" Xorphiul asked.

"I just can't. It's as if there is a barrier there. But sometimes there are ways around it. For example, since the meeting hall is technically a part of the sewer, there is nothing preventing me from going there, either. Or the alcove at Cromsen where I hid Jack, since it doesn't belong to anyone."

"Wait, you hid Jack?"

"Oh right, you haven't heard the whole story," Enya said. "Nole was the one Rhyn hired to kidnap Jack, but the Black Matron took him away before we found Nole and made him take us to the hiding spot."

"So, why are you even here now?" he asked the vampire.

Nole shrugged and winced, nearly stumbling. "Ouch!"

"What?" Enya asked, latching onto his shoulders to keep from falling into the water.

"Your sword's handle zapped me when it touched me."

"Oh. Sorry."

"I can carry her, if it helps," Xorphiul

offered.

"If you'd like. She's shockingly lighter than she looks."

"Thanks," Enya muttered.

She was passed off to her brother's arms, carefully to ensure the sword handle didn't touch either of the men, and they continued sloshing through the calf-high water.

"What were we talking about?" Nole asked.

"I asked why you were even here, if you were the one who kidnapped Jack."

"Oh, right. I have nothing against Jack—I was just doing what I was paid to do. But I owe it to Enya. And she'll blast me to bits if I don't help her."

Xorphiul gave Enya a shocked look and she shrugged, nearly bumping him with the hilt as well.

"Something like that."

Nole stopped by a wall and pushed a spot about eye level. Part of the wall moved open and he ducked inside, out of the water, to find several other people already inside. All eyes were on him, as were more than one sword.

"It's just me!" He held up his hands.

"Nole?" The startled exclamation came

from a few of those present before they all were distracted by the others who bumped into him when he did not move past the doorway.

"Is that a satyr?" someone asked.

"And that's a naiad! They're the ones they're after!"

"They're with me," Nole shouted over those and the other cries.

"You haven't been here for ages," a female vampire said, stepping closer. "And they'll call off the zombies if they're turned in."

"If you hand them over to Rhyn, he'll just take them to the Black Matron where they'll revive all of the Maven, and it'll be even worse than some revived elves." He threw a glance over his shoulder to Xorphiul, who put Enya down on the damp but flood-free ground. "No offense."

Enya gasped. "Oh no!"

"What is it?" Xorphiul asked.

"I just realized, the elves are the only ones affected, the dead ones were revived, and Rhyn's controlling them—which means they must have used the spell they plan to use on us on Jack!" She gasped again. "You don't think they would have had to kill him to do that, do you?"

"I honestly have no idea how it works," Xorphiul said.

"I doubt Rhyn would have gone to all that trouble to train you just so he could kill you," Nole said. "He probably hoped you would fight alongside him."

"Why on Terra would I do that?"

"Well, I have a feeling he wasn't exactly expecting things to be revealed the way they were."

"Um, we should probably deal with this later," Xorphiul said, gesturing to the group of trained former Resistance fighters who had moved much closer while they were all talking.

"The point is," Nole addressed them once more, "you don't want to turn them in. It'll just make everything ten times worse."

"Can you start from the beginning?" a troll[34] asked, scratching his head.

Nole turned to Enya. "Do you want to tell, or should I?"

"They're your friends."

"Right." He faced the group again. "The Black Matron is working with a satyr named

---

[34] similar to ogres, but turn to stone in sunlight and frequent bridges

Rhyn. He must have known about the twins," he held a thumb over his shoulder at them in case anyone had not caught the fact that Enya and Xorphiul were, in fact, twins, "and for some reason they're apparently the key in this spell that will revive the Mavens, but under Rhyn and the Black Matron's control.

"Anyway, Rhyn went looking for the twins, and he found Enya, but Xorphiul had been switched with an elf changeling in infancy, so Rhyn knew Jack, the elf who everyone said was Enya's brother, wasn't really her brother. So he hired me—I had taken up work as a mercenary—to kidnap Jack in order to force Enya to find the djinn's lamp and wish for her brother so her real brother, Xor, would show up instead, only I didn't recognize Rhyn when I saw him again because he'd cloaked himself with magic and, well, a cloak."

"Is all this really necessary?" the other vampire asked, tapping her foot impatiently.

"Yes. The point is, Jack, whom Enya still considers a brother, is being held captive by the Black Matron, likely the trigger to the elf zombie curse, and we need to get him away from there without them getting their hands on the twins, as I feel I've made myself clear what happens if they do."

"So you do want to go to the Black Matron, just on your own terms."

"Exactly. We were actually hoping maybe the Resistance could come back together and help us with that part."

"You know what happened the last time we tried."

"This time it's different. This time we have Enya. She has an enormous amount of magic, but she needs to learn how to fight first. If she and the Resistance work together, we might actually have a chance with this."

"Just how powerful is she?" the vampire asked, eyeing Enya skeptically.

"I turned the entire Lake Lucid into one giant tidal wave," Enya answered, rolling her shoulders back and lifting her nose up.

"All of it?" the vampire asked, her eyes widening as murmurs spread among the rest of them.

"Yes. So you might as well not even try to turn us in." Enya crossed her arms. "You probably couldn't subdue me even if you wanted to."

"The Black Matron herself is another

matter, however," Nole jumped in. "So what's it going to be then?"

"This is quite a big deal," the vampire said. "We have to discuss it amongst ourselves."

They backed away and moved into a circle to debate how they wanted to proceed.

"Who is she?" Enya asked quietly while they waited for the answer.

"Pel. Pel Para.The unofficial leader, were they to become a group again. The real leader was killed by the Black Matron. Yet another reason for the disbanding."

"If you disbanded so long ago, why were they all here?" Xorphiul asked.

"This is probably the safest place in the city. I doubt it was planned. They just all had the same idea I did. Works in our favor, if they agree. We won't have to waste time gathering them."

"All right, we've made up our minds," Pel announced as the circle dissolved. "We certainly don't want the Black Matron to rule, so we're not going to turn you two over. It's not worth the risk."

"Oh, good." Xorphiul sighed in relief.

"We also want to stop this zombie curse. And... if what you said about Enya's magic is true, then this seems like our best chance at defeating them."

"So you'll help us?" Enya asked.

Pel nodded. "Yes. As of now, the Resistance is officially reinstated."

9 - Preparation

IT WASN'T EASY training in the cramped secret sewer room, but with the elves haunting the ground floor, they had little choice. Or so they thought.

"Maybe it's time to seek other options," Jaro, the seraph[35] training Enya on how to use her sword, suggested. "We keep having to reel ourselves in. This is no way to learn the art of sword fighting."

"What other option is there?" Pel said. "The zombies roam the streets."

"We could leave through the drain," Jaro said. "It'll take us beyond the city. We can venture even further once we're out there to put distance between us and them, but then we can spread out."

It sounded like a much better plan than being cramped into a small—at least for a

---

[35] celestial warrior with six wings; because two couldn't possibly be sufficient

dozen creatures of varying shapes and sizes—smelly old sewer passageway, so they clambered to do as he suggested.

"I can't touch the water, or whatever you want to call that, though," Enya said.

"I can carry you again," Xorphiul offered.

With her permission, he scooped her in his arms and headed through the sewers with the others. The rumble of rushing water grew steadily louder as they went, but before they reached the drain, Xorphiul jumped, jostling Enya about.

"Something brushed past my leg."

"Don't worry," Jaro said from where he flew above the water's surface. "There shouldn't be anything living down here. It was probably just some refuse."

"Why don't you come down here and check for yourself," Xorphiul muttered under his breath.

"Sorry, I didn't catch that," Jaro said.

"Nothing."

He kept walking until something wound rapidly up his left leg, tripping him. Enya flew from his grasp and straight into the water, transforming instantly.

"It's a kraken[36]!" Mnor, the troll, yelled, stomping through the water away from Xorphiul.

Enya could see for herself as she adjusted to her new surroundings. She was able to see through the water better than when she was above its surface. The beast had flattened itself down to be unseen by those who passed by, using its tentacles to sneak up on them. It wound a tentacle around the legs of two more companions, dragging them and Xorphiul back toward its crab-like mouth.

The now-familiar pulse surged throughout Enya and rippled through the water toward the kraken. Instead of harming it, she just managed to anger it and it turned its attention to her. As three tentacles lashed at her, she used her magic to quickly cool the liquid surrounding the creature until it froze it in place.

Popping up to the surface, she checked in on the others. Two of them, including Xorphiul, had gotten their legs trapped in the ice she had made. Sighing, she moved

---

[36] water monster with long tentacles and a face only a mother could love

closer and chose to melt the spots they stood in. It worked like a charm[37] while leaving the kraken still frozen solid.

"Huh," Pel said, flying along the ceiling to see the damage. "Impressive."

"Thank you." Enya sent the thought to her through magic. She was really getting the hang of all of this. She was not, however, getting the hang of being submerged in utter filth. With newfound determination, she shot along the tunnels, using the current to guide and propel her toward the drain. Almost before she knew it, she was pouring out over it along with the rest of the water and landed in a pool outside of the town under the night sky. She quickly headed to the bank and was soon back in her usual form. "Ugh, I'm never doing that again."

"You never know," Nole said. He had followed Pel and Jaro's examples and flown the whole time, and now he landed beside her as dry as she was. "I mean, you weren't exactly planning on doing it the first time, either. These things have a way of happening."

"They wouldn't if I was home, minding my

---

[37] which is good, since it was a charm

own business."

The others began making their appearances, some by flying and others by the less sanitary route. By the time Xorphiul made it to shore, he was covered in slime and rubbing at his arms.

"I have never needed a bath so desperately in my entire life."

"There's a river up north," Nole said. "It's the source from which the city obtains its water supply. Besides, we'd have to cross it anyway. Might as well get to it now."

"Of course there would be even more water involved." Enya's huffs had slowly started to become sighs of resignation.

The group journeyed a short distance to the river, the others just as thrilled as Xorphiul was to bathe. Once clean, they spent the rest of the night teaching Enya much more in depth versions of the lessons she had been getting with Rhyn. As she did, Pel approached Nole.

"How have you been?"

He fiddled with a loose thread on the edge of his cloak. "Making do. I've found some work as a mercenary, so I get by."

She raised an eyebrow. "That's not what I meant."

He sighed. "I know. I'm fine." He looked up at her. "How about you?"

"Same as ever."

They watched Enya and Jaro spar for a moment.

"I can't say I expected this one, though," Pel said. "You showing up, asking us to reinstate the Resistance and take on the Black Matron."

"I know. I hadn't expected it either. I just took a job and next thing I knew I was here. If I'd known the job would put the whole world in danger of being overtaken by the Black Matron and zombie Mavens, I would never have agreed to it in the first place."

Pel looked him over. "Are you really sure about this? You're not going to flake out again this time, right?"

Nole stared at the ground. "It's different now. This time if we fail, the whole world suffers." He wanted to assure her that this meant he would not flake out like she said, but he knew he could not make that promise.

Enya quickly earned the respect of those in the Resistance.

"I've never seen such natural talent,"

Giolo, the ifrit[38] sorceress, said as morning neared.

"I did wish for control over my magic," Enya said, trying not to feel as proud as she was. "It's made things incredibly easier."

"It's not just the magic," Giolo said. "You're a natural at everything."

"It's because she was born to be a Maven," Jaro said.

The huffs were back. "I don't want to be a Maven. I just want to get Jack without dying, or turning into their trigger."

"I thought we didn't want the Maven back," Mnor said.

"Just not the ones who are supposed to be dead and will be controlled through magic to do the Rhyn's bidding," Nole clarified.

"Oh..." Mnor looked more confused than before but did not ask any more questions.

"If I'm such a natural, when do you think we'll be ready to storm the castle?" Enya asked Pel.

"We can at least start heading there

---

[38] related to djinns, a winged fire being of magic who typically lives underground; unlike djinns, they do not grant wishes, unless your wish is to be burned alive in a tunnel

tonight. Maybe by the time we reach it, you'll be ready."

❦

"How much did Nole tell you about what happened before?"

The sun had crept into view, and the vampires and Mnor were hidden away in an underground cavern Giolo created for them. The others also prepared to rest for the day, but Jaro had pulled Enya aside.

"Not much, just that the Black Matron killed several of your group, including the one Nole had joined to impress."

Jaro nodded. "May I ask why you teamed up with him now?"

"He was our best chance at tracking down Jack, so I made him come with me to make up for kidnapping him in the first place."

"I see." Jaro's eyes darted to the entrance to the cavern. "Just don't expect him to be of much use once we reach the castle."

Enya narrowed her eyes. "What do you mean?"

"As much as he cared about Rillion, it did

not prevent him from fleeing when it was time for them to attack. I doubt it would have made much of a difference in the grand scheme of things—if she took down the others, he never would have stood a chance—but he still abandoned them at a crucial moment to save himself."

"That's not all that surprising." Enya shrugged. "He told me his main focus was self-preservation. And from what I've seen, he's more tactical than brave."

"Then so long as you're aware. I would not want you to go into this relying on him to get you through it."

"I think between the strategies you and Giolo have shown me and the Resistance backing me up, we should make it just fine."

"I like your confidence." Jaro gave her a thin smile.

"Nole didn't really elaborate on Rillion. Who was he?"

"He was a puca[39], and our leader."

Enya widened her eyes. "He was the leader?"

Jaro nodded. "Nole only joined to support

---

[39] shapeshifting magical creature, often appearing in the form of a six-foot, three-and-a-half inch tall rabbit

him. He never cared about the actual mission, never paid attention to any of the briefings. He wanted Rillion to believe he was brave without actually doing anything to prove it."

"What did Rillion think?"

"He could tell what was going on, so he decided to bring Nole along in hopes it would help spur him to become the man he should have been. It didn't work."

"Well, like I said, we should be set with or without him."

◆

"The most important part," Pel said as they made their final plans outside the castle, "is that they're expecting the twins at some point, so we have to be ready to be noticed right away. They don't know about us though, so we still have some elements of surprise."

"We should just leave Xorphiul out of this," Jaro said. "That way if something goes wrong, they won't be able to finish their spell."

"No!" Xorphiul cried. When everyone gave him shocked looks, he cleared his throat. "I mean, I want to help. This is my sister's mission. I need to be there for her."

"I agree with Jaro," Pel said. "It's too risky to have you both inside. And you don't have much to offer to help."

"But—"

"Xor, it's all right," Enya said, putting a hand on his shoulder. "The last thing I want is for you to be captured, too. It's bad enough they already have Jack. Wait here for us."

"But what if something happens to you? Don't you get it? You're all I have now."

Enya's expression fell. "You have to trust me. I'll be fine. You wouldn't be able to help even if you were there. I'm doing this to protect you."

Xorphiul looked away. It wasn't fair. Even when she was disappointing him, she was still looking out for him. He had to make sure she wasn't hurt. His hand moved to the side of his robe concealing the lamp. Yes, he would stay here. As soon as everyone was out of sight, he would see to it that she was safe.

"Jack is most likely in the dungeons," Pel

said, bringing the focus back to the plan. "From our intel last time, the best route should be for Giolo to make a tunnel on the eastern side to bring you there. Unfortunately, I cannot go inside without permission, so I'll stay back with the outside team."

"Oh, right," Nole said. "I suppose I can't go inside either." This thought had occurred to him a long time ago, but he had been waiting for a chance to bring it up without seeming too eager. In fact, before things had turned out as they had, he had originally planned to use the excuse to get out of joining Enya in the end.

Enya leveled her gaze on him. She had thought a lot about what Jaro said, and was just as content with this solution as Nole was. "You should stay by Xor, in case any trouble comes his way."

Nole nodded, knowing she was just trying to make him feel useful without saying as much.

Pel assigned everyone their positions, and they decided there was no reason not to get started now. As they checked their gear and prepared themselves, Enya approached Xorphiul.

"I don't usually do this, but... Just in case." She gave him a quick hug. "I'll be back with Jack before you know it, and then this whole mess will be over and we can go to the farm together. I know it's a big change for you, but it's a really nice place. I think you'll like it once you get used to it."

Xorphiul smiled. "I'm sure I will." He grew more serious. "But please, be careful."

"I will," she promised and turned to Nole. "Watch out for him, all right? Once they realize we're here, one of them might come looking for him, too, so be on the alert."

"Of course."

Enya left with the Resistance, everyone scattering into position, while Nole and Xorphiul hung back, hidden in the trees but able to see a little of the castle. Xorphiul casually watched Nole out of the corner of his eye. He wasn't entirely sure why he felt the need to ensure the lamp was still secret, but he figured he would avoid a lot of pesky questions that way. As he waited for the vampire to become distracted, he tried to work out the best wish.

Perhaps it was time to simply wish Jack away. Then Enya would no longer need to go into the castle at all. But... the more

Xorhpiul thought about it, the less he wanted Jack to be rescued at all. Sure, Enya was kind to him now, but once Jack was back, things would be different. And Jack wasn't even her real brother, like he was. If anyone deserved her sisterly affection, it was him. No, what he really needed was for them to fail—but without getting hurt in the process. Perhaps fail was not the right word. He needed them to give up before they got too far. A grim smile spread across his face. He knew exactly what to wish for, if only that blasted bat[40] would move away.

Realizing that Nole would follow Enya's instructions and refuse to leave him until it was too late, Xorphiul decided he would have to use the lamp regardless. Nole would notice soon enough either way. Stepping back so he was not directly in Nole's line of view—he was at least focused enough on the castle to not find this odd—Xorphiul untied his robe and reached for the lamp, finally following through and rubbing the side this time. Green smoke poured out into the shape of the djinn.

---

[40] oddly enough, bats do not exist in this world, but rather are mythological creatures inspired by vampires

"What is your first wish?"

Nole spun around. "Wait, what? You had the lamp this whole time?"

Xorphiul ignored him. "I wish Enya would forget about—" at the last second, he remembered how the djinn had mixed him and Jack up during Enya's wish; he would leave no room for error this time, "—the elf she considers a brother."

"What? No!" Nole cried, but it was too late.

Green smoke flew from the djinn in the direction Enya had gone.

10 - The Curse

GREEN SMOKE SURROUNDED Enya just as they exited Giolo's tunnel into the dungeons.

"It's a trap!" Mnor yelled.

"Shush!" Jaro shushed him when he saw the smoke dissipate almost immediately.

Enya blinked. "Wait, what are we doing here?"

"What are you talking about?" Jaro frowned. "This was your idea."

"But we just walked right into the Black Matron's lair for no reason! I'm getting out of here."

"What—"

Before Jaro could finish the thought, the tunnel collapsed behind them, shaking the ground so hard it threw them all off their feet.

"It's a trap!" Mnor repeated.

"Be quiet!" Jaro snapped.

"I don't think he's in the dungeons after all," Giolo said, moving through the hallway, the light from her flaming body illuminating the dim cells.

"Who isn't?" Enya asked.

"Jack," Jaro said.

"Who?"

"What is wrong with you?" Jaro rounded on her and scrutinized her face. "What did that green smoke do to you?"

Enya stepped back and crossed her arms. "I have no idea what you're talking about."

"Enya, you have to snap out of this," Jaro said. "Or at least do something about the Black Matron. We're counting on you."

"To do what exactly? She's the Black Matron of Death! Why on Terra did we ever come here?"

"To get Jack!"

"Who's Jack?" Enya huffed. She was getting really annoyed that no one was making any sense, and could not understand why Jaro kept talking about some guy with a bizarre name.

"Your brother!"

Enya shook her head as her forehead crinkled. "My brother's name is Xorphiul."

"No, your other brother, the one we risked everything to break out of here so we could stop the elf zombie curse."

"What does he have to do with the zombie curse?"

"Gah, never mind," Jaro waved a hand. "This is pointless. Just fight the Black Matron when we find her, all right?"

"And get myself killed? I don't think so."

The dungeons slammed open.

"It's her!" Giolo cried.

"Enya, please," Jaro hissed. "Don't leave us to die."

Light streamed down the stairway from the open door, and a black shadow made its way down the stairs. Enya turned to the fallen tunnel they had come through and sent magic to clear it once more.

"Go!" she cried.

Mnor was the first to charge through it, and Enya was right on his heels, though not for long. She froze in place as a magic barrier tightened around her. Though her back was to the others, based on Mnor's body, stuck in mid-step, she assumed they had all been caught in the Black Matron's magic. She heard footsteps approaching, and a black figure moved in front of her, though the lighting was too dim to make out any details. The Black Matron grabbed Enya's hair and yanked her to the side, causing her to cry out in pain. She still could not move as the Black Matron pulled her along the hallway to the stairs before waving her hand behind them. The entire dungeon collapsed on the frozen Resistance.

◆

"Why would you do that?" Nole cried.

"It's for the best," Xorphiul said.

"The best? What in Dracula's name are you talking about?"

"I'm trying to keep her safe."

"Safe? Are you insane? There's a horde of zombie elves roaming the land. If we don't get Jack out of there now, no one will be safe!"

Xorphiul swished his tail. "They don't turn other creatures besides elves."

"But they do eat them!"

"Oh. Right."

"Do you have a second wish or can I return to the lamp?" the djinn asked.

Nole lunged for Xorphiul, trying to snatch the lamp away, but it was still tied to his belt. They hit the ground.

"Get off!" Xorphiul cried as they wrestled for the lamp.

"Take it back!" Nole shouted.

"No!"

"Then give it to me!"

"No!"

Nole's sharp nails clawed through the cord and the lamp bounced a few feet away. Both men went to grab it and froze.

"I'll just take that for safe keeping," Rhyn said as he stepped into view and scooped up the lamp. "Now, it certainly took you long enough to get here."

He grabbed Xorphiul's outstretched arm and pulled him away, knocking Nole over in the process. "Thanks for all of your help, Nole. I couldn't have done this without you."

Nole grimaced but, try as he might, he could not break free from the magical restraints. He could only watch as Rhyn dragged Xorphiul away. As they neared the castle entryway, Pel swooped in to attack, but Rhyn released his grip on Xorphiul and parried. Pel was no match for a Maven master, but Rhyn's distraction did allow Nole to be freed.

And then he hesitated. Seeing Pel and Rhyn battling made everything within him want to run the other way, but he knew he couldn't. Rhyn was right. He had handed Jack over and led the twins right into their trap, and if left alone, Pel would be dead soon, and who knew what fate the rest of the Resistance faced? Speaking of, where were the others who were supposed to be watching the castle?

Nole sniffed about and froze. He had been so distracted by Xor and the lamp, he had not noticed the fresh blood coming from each position. Pel must have been the only one Rhyn had not assassinated on his way.

He turned his attention back to the fight and saw one of Pel's wings was wounded, and she struggled to stay aloft. Gritting his teeth, Nole dashed through the trees until he reached open ground and spread his wings, propelling himself at Rhyn. The satyr twisted and stabbed him in the gut with one of his daggers. Nole grunted and slumped to the ground. Well, that certainly did not go as planned.

Pel breathed heavily as she darted in for one last attack, but she was too weakened by now. Rhyn dodged and finished her off with a stab to the neck. The vampire landed in a heap near Nole, the scent of her dark blood filling Nole's nostrils.

Rhyn shook his head at Nole as he wiped his blades clean. "I really don't know why she insisted on bringing you. You're so pathetic."

He reached for Xorphiul again and pulled him the rest of the way into the castle. Nole lay on his back, putting pressure on the wound, and closed his eyes. Rhyn was right yet again. Even as the pain began to lessen and a rough scab formed over the wound—it would be fully healed within a day—Nole could not bring himself to move. What was the point? He would never be a hero. It was not his lot in life. He might as well have just turned tail and ran like last time. Nothing he did changed the fate of the twins or the Resistance anyway. He was nothing but a pathetic, wimpy failure.

♦

The Black Matron and Rhyn brought the twins into the throne room at the same time. Jack hovered with his eyes closed, a purple glow surrounding him, but Enya just wondered what that was all about.

Moving each of them to a spot on the floor where a detailed design was drawn, the Black Matron and Rhyn stepped back.

"Go ahead," Rhyn said.

The Black Matron nodded and began concocting the spell. As she did so, purple fog seeped from her and surrounded the twins, lifting them in the same way as Jack.

Meanwhile, by what was formerly Lake Lucid, a rumbling filled the ground, and within moments the Maven had returned to Terra. The satyrs were hardly more than skeletons, and the nymphs largely globs of whatever element they had once been, but they soon developed into recognizable physical forms. They scattered, their intention to divide and conquer—or rather, the Black Matron's intention, for they had no will of their own.

Back at the castle, Enya was lost to all thought and awareness. All she knew was that she was connected to a group of beings somewhere in the distance, but she could hardly fathom what it meant, and could not be bothered to care enough to figure it out.

♦

Nole sat up. He was being ridiculous. If he just sat here, he'd be proving everyone right. He had already let Pel and the others die. He was the only one the enemy were no longer factoring in. It was all up to him to save the twins, and Jack, and the rest of the world.

Taking in a few deep breaths first, he pushed himself to his feet and stumbled toward the castle. He may heal rather swiftly, but it still hurt when he moved. The more he pressed on, the easier it became to ignore the pain, but he still needed a plan. More specifically, he needed a plan to reach the lamp. Rhyn could bind him with magic if he was aware of Nole's presence, so he needed some way to get to him without being noticed. But how?

Spreading his wings once more, he glided around as he followed the scents to the throne room behind a second story window. He saw Enya, Xor, and Jack all levitating in the midst of their purple fog and frowned.

"Moentae." The strange word rang through his head. He could not recall ever hearing it before, and had no idea what it meant, but

there it was.

Shaking the thought from his head, he focused on the task at hand. Pulling in a few deep breaths, he reared and charged at the window, holding his arms in front of him as he crashed through the glass and flew straight into Rhyn.

"Enya!" he called as he jumped after the lamp that skidded away. "Wake up!"

He grabbed the lamp just as the Black Matron finally reacted and cast the binding spell around him, but his hand was upon it and he was still able to rub the side of it with his thumb. The djinn began to materialize again, and he realized he had forgotten to think of a wish to use, so he blurted out the first thing that came to mind before she had the chance to ask what he wished for.

"I wish the wish just used on Enya was undone!"

Once again, the green smoke surrounded Enya, mixing with the purple fog.

Enya opened her eyes. She had heard a voice calling her name, begging her to wake up, though she hadn't realized she was asleep. And then something had clicked within her. Jack. She needed to save Jack.

When her eyes opened, she took in her surroundings. Rhyn and the Black Matron were facing her, watching as the green smoke faded.

"But a wish like that shouldn't have allowed her to wake up," Rhyn said, eyes wide.

Enya looked down and saw that she was floating in a sea of purple, then noticed both of her brothers were in the same predicament. Rage drew her brow down and she threw her hands out, dispersing the fog around her and dropping to the floor.

"Impossible!" Rhyn subconsciously backed away.

Enya reached out toward her brothers and their fog vanished as well, sending them crashing to the floor significantly less gracefully than it had her, for they were still rather unaware of anything. The collision broke that spell, however, and they both stirred.

"But, how...?" Rhyn was at a loss for words.

"She wished for control over magic," the djinn explained, examining her nails and seeming all around unimpressed by anything happening in the room.

"Wait, you mean I have control over other

people's magic, too?" Enya asked.

The djinn shrugged. "I just did what you wished for."

Jack groaned, putting a hand to his head, and Enya rushed to his side.

"Are you all right?"

"Enya!" He threw his arms around her. "I didn't think you'd actually come!"

"Of course I came," she snapped, pulling away. "What do you take me for?"

Rhyn took advantage of her distraction to charge at her, daggers in hand, but Sauveur flew into Enya's hand. She twirled without even thinking, following Jaro's instructions, and ran him through. The daggers came within a hair's breadth of her cheek before coming to a stop, Enya's blade jutting through his chest and out his back. She was as surprised as he was.

"No," he moaned, then gave a strangled cough, and the light faded from his eyes.

Enya dropped the sword, sending Rhyn's body to the floor, but Sauveur pulled itself free and slammed into her hand again. Grimacing at the sight of the blood, she felt she had no choice but to face their other adversary and turned on the dark figure.

"I wish the Black Matron could not hurt

us."

The smoke moved to the Black Matron in response to Nole's words. She did not move or speak as it wrapped around her before diminishing. Instead, she simply turned and walked away and out the door as they watched her. Nole hit the floor as the magic binding him was suddenly released.

"Oof!"

"Thank you." Enya approached him and knelt beside him. "For everything. You really saved the day here."

"Oh, I don't know about that. I mean... You think so?"

"I was lost in that spell until you helped me." She offered him a hand, which he accepted, and she pulled him to his feet.

"I'd say it was nothing, but... I'm actually rather shocked I did all that."

She tilted her head. "Wait, how did you get inside?"

Nole hesitated, rubbing his neck. "I'm not sure... To be honest, I completely forgot about that obstacle at the time. I just knew I needed to get inside, so I went for it."

Before they could come up with an explanation, Enya spotted Xorphiul, the only one she had not yet spoken to. He stood, glumly looking at his hands as he twiddled his thumbs.

"Xor? You all right?"

He peeked up at her. "You're not mad at me?"

Enya frowned. "Why would I be mad at you?"

The wish having been undone, she had forgotten all about her momentary memory loss. Hope sparked within Xorphiul as he realized there was no need for her to ever know the truth.

"Um, because I let myself get captured," he supplied.

Nole narrowed his eyes at the young satyr but did not refute his statement. Enya had gone through so much trouble on her brother's behalf; it would not be fair to turn her against her other brother—assuming Xorphiul wouldn't cause any more trouble. He'd have to keep an eye on him.

Enya shrugged. "So did the rest of us. But it's all over now. We can finally go home. Well, to our home. I hope you'll consider it such before long."

Xorphiul nodded with a small smile. While he still was not fond of the notion of living on a farm, and having to share Enya with Jack, at least he would be with his family.

"Um, Enya?" Jack piped up.

"Yes?"

"What's going on exactly?"

11 - The End?

IT TOOK QUITE a bit of explaining to catch Jack up to speed with everything that had happened, but eventually he more or less got the gist. He was rather bummed he would never get the chance to meet his real parents, but the gnome farm had always been home to him anyway.

As they prepared to set out on the start of one final journey, Enya pulled Nole aside.

"Have you figured out what you're going to use that last wish for yet?" she asked.

He shook his head. "I think I'll save it for later. Just in case. You never know when zombie elves are going to show up again."

"They better not." She tapped her fingers against her other hand. "So, what are you going to do now?"

"Go back to Cromsen, I guess."

She nodded. "Good luck out there."

Nole grinned and started to walk away, but paused and turned. "You know, when we first met, I thought you were a pain. But I know now that you never would have blasted me to smithereens, and you're really something. If I actually was interested in females, you might be in the running."

Enya rolled her eyes. "When I first met you, I thought you were a wimp, but you really aren't. And even though I am interested in males, you still aren't my type."

Nole chuckled at that. "Well, so long as we're on the same page. If you ever need anything, you know where to find me."

"Oh, I doubt I'll ever be that desperate. I plan to live a mild life from now on."

"Sure. Living a mild life with a sword that refuses to leave your side."

"Right, I forgot about that." She pulled the sword free and examined it more closely than she had before. "I wonder why that is. It would be nice to just be rid of it. Do you think my control over magic would allow me to put it down for good?"

"I have no idea, but it's worth a try." He frowned at the blade. "What does it say there?"

She followed his pointing finger to the small inscription along the base of the blade by the hilt. It read, *"Only the Savior of Terra may yield."*

"The Savior of Terra?" Enya frowned. "As in, how we just saved Terra from undead Maven and elves?"

"Well, we did let the Black Matron go free. And there's always that Thero guy Rhyn mentioned, the one in charge of all of this."

Enya huffed. "Blast. Why is nothing ever simple?"

We hope you enjoyed reading
Satyr Wars: A Naiad Hope by
Becca Bates. Please consider
visiting your favorite online
venue to post a review!

To find more exciting and
engaging books, please visit
Indie Artist Press at
www.indieartistpress.com.

About the Author

Becca Bates was born in August 1990 in southern California. From an early age, she was an avid reader and often created stories of her own, though it wasn't until high school that she began writing her first novel.

After writing for a few years as a side hobby, her love for it grew until she decided it was her greatest passion and something worth pursuing professionally.

She makes her home in Fort Collins, Colorado.

You can contact Becca at:
http://beccabates.weebly.com

Free Ebook!

Once upon a time...

Get your free ebook copy of
"Faerie Tail" by signing up
for Becca Bates' newletter.
Start Here:
http://beccabooks.weebly.com